COSMIC CONSPIRACY

"In A.D. 2560 Earth had become the world of null-A, or non-Aristotelianism, controlled by a gigantic Games Machine, made up of twenty-five thousand electronic brains. . . . Gilbert Gosseyn came to the Games Machine that year, only to find that he didn't know who he was, and, even more amazing, that he could be killed and still live, in his own original body!

"Later, Gosseyn learned that he was evidently a pawn in an astral game some super-brain was playing to thwart an attack on the solar system from outer space. Mr. van Vogt's novel shuttles back and forth between Venus and Earth, and the story is packed with Hitchcockian action. . . . The science-fiction fan, whose name has become legion in recent years, will hail it as the classic of the year."

—*New York Herald Tribune*

by the same author

THE PLAYERS OF NULL-A
SLAN

by A. E. Van Vogt & E. Mayne Hull
THE WINGED MAN

The World of Null-A

This edition revised
and with an introduction by the author
A. E. van Vogt

A BERKLEY MEDALLION BOOK
published by
BERKLEY PUBLISHING CORPORATION

Berkley Publishing Corporation
200 Madison Avenue
New York, N.Y. 10016

SBN 425-03322-8

BERKLEY MEDALLION BOOKS are published by
Berkley Publishing Corporation
200 Madison Avenue
New York, N.Y. 10016

BERKLEY MEDALLION BOOK ® TM 757,375

Printed in the United States of America

Berkley Medallion Edition, JANUARY, 1977

FOURTH PRINTING

AUTHOR'S INTRODUCTION

Reader, in your hands you hold one of the most controversial—and successful—novels in the whole of science fiction literature.

In these introductory remarks, I am going to tell about some of the successes and I shall also detail what the principal critics said about *The World of Null-A*. Let me hasten to say that what you shall read is no acrimonious defense. In fact, I have decided to take the criticisms seriously, and I have accordingly revised this first Berkley edition and have provided the explanations which for so long I believed to be unnecessary.

Before I tell you of the attacks, I propose swiftly to set down a few of *The World of Null-A*'s successes:

It was the first hard-cover science fiction novel published by a major publisher after World War II (Simon and Schuster, 1948).

It won the Manuscripters Club award.

It was listed by the New York area library association among the hundred best novels of 1948.

Jacques Sadoul, in France, editor of *Editions OPTA*, has stated that *World of Null-A*, when first published, all by itself created the French science fiction market. The first edition sold over 25,000 copies. He has stated that I am still—in 1969—the most popular writer in France in terms of copies sold.

Its publication stimulated interest in General Semantics. Students flocked to the Institute of General Semantics, Lakewood, Connecticut, to study under Count Alfred Korzybski—who allowed himself to be photographed reading *The World of Null-A*. Today, General Semantics, then a faltering science, is taught in hundreds of universities.

World has been translated into nine languages.

With that out of the way, we come to the attacks. As you'll see, they're more fun, make authors madder, and get readers stirred up.

Here is what Sam Moskowitz, in his brief biography of the author, said in his book, *Seekers of Tomorrow*, about what was wrong with *World of Null-A:* ". . . Bewildered Gilbert Gosseyn, mutant with a double mind, doesn't know who he is and spends the entire novel trying to find out." The novel was originally printed as a serial in *Astounding Science Fiction*, and after the final installment was published (Mr. Moskowitz continues), "Letters of plaintive puzzlement began to pour in. Readers didn't understand what the story was all about. Campbell [the editor advised them to wait a few days; it took that long, he suggested, for the implications to sink in. The days turned into months, but clarification never came—"

You'll admit that's a tough set of sentences to follow. Plain, blunt-spoken Sam Moskowitz, whose knowledge of science fiction history and whose collection of science fiction probably is topped only by that of Forrest Ackerman (in the whole universe) . . . is nevertheless in error. The number of readers who wrote "plaintive" letters to the editor can be numbered on the fingers of one and a half hands.

However, Moskowitz might argue that it isn't the quantity of complainers, but the quality. And there he has a point.

Shortly after *The World of Null-A* was serialized in 1945, a sci-fi fan, hitherto unknown to me, wrote in a science fiction fan magazine a long and powerful article attacking the novel and my work in general up to that time. The article concluded, as I recall it (from memory only) with the sentence: "Van Vogt is actually a pygmy writer working with a giant typewriter."

The imagery throughout this article, meaningless though that particular line is (if you'll think about it), induced me to include in my answering article in a subsequent issue of the same fan magazine—which article is lost to posterity—the remark that I foresaw a brilliant writing career for the young man who had written so poetical an attack.

That young writer eventually developed into the science fictional genius, Damon Knight, who—among his many accomplishments—a few years ago organized the Science Fiction Writers of America, which (though it seems impossible) is still a viable organization.

Of Knight's attack so long ago, *Galaxy Magazine* critic Algis Budrys wrote in his December, 1967, book review column: "In this edition [of critical essays] you will find among other goodies from the earlier version, the famous destruction of A. E. van Vogt that made Damon's reputation."

What other criticisms of *The World of Null-A* are there? None. It's a fact. Singlehandedly, Knight took on this novel and my work at age 23-1/2, and, as Algis Budrys puts it, brought about my "destruction."

So what's the problem? Why am I now revising *World*? Am I doing all this for *one* critic?

Yep.

But why?—you ask.

Well, on this planet you have to recognize where the power is.

Knight has it?

Knight has it.

In a deeper sense, of course, I'm making this defense of the book, and revising it, because General Semantics is a worthwhile subject, with meaningful implications, not only in 2560 A.D. where my story takes place, but here and now.

General Semantics, as defined by the late Count Alfred Korzybski in his famous book, *Science and Sanity,* is an over-word for non-Aristotelian and non-Newtonian systems. Don't let that mouthful of words stop you. Non-Aristotelian means not according to the thought solidified by Aristotle's followers for nearly 2,000 years. Non-Newtonian refers to our essentially Einsteinian universe, as accepted by today's science. Non-Aristotelian breaks down to Non-A, and then Null-A.

Thus, the titles *World of*—and *Players of*—*Null-A.*

General Semantics has to do with the Meaning of Meaning. In this sense, it transcends and encompasses the new science of Linguistics. The essential idea of General

Semantics is that meaning can only be comprehended when one has made allowances for the nervous and perception system—that of a human being—through which it is filtered.

Because of the limitations of his nervous system, Man can only see part of truth, never the whole of it. In describing the limitation, Korzybski coined the term "ladder of abstraction." Abstraction, as he used it, did not have a lofty or symbolical thought connotation. It meant, "to abstract from", that is, to take from something a part of the whole. His assumption: in observing a process of nature, one can only abstract—i.e. perceive—a portion of it.

Now, if I were a writer who merely presented another man's ideas, then I doubt if I'd have had problems with my readers. I think I presented the facts of General Semantics so well, and so skilfully, in *World of Null-A* and its sequel that the readers thought that that was all I *should* be doing. But the truth is that I, the author, saw a deeper paradox.

Ever since Einstein's theory of relativity, we have had the concept of the observer who—it was stated—must be taken into account. Whenever I discussed this with people, I observed they were not capable of appreciating the height of that concept. They seemed to think of the observer as, essentially, an algebraic unit. Who he was didn't matter.

In such sciences as chemistry and physics, so precise were the methods that, apparently, *it did not matter* who the observer was. Japanese, Germans, Russians, Catholics, Protestants, Hindus, and Englishmen all arrived at the same impeccable conclusions, apparently bypassing their personal, racial, and religious prejudices. However, everyone I talked to was aware that, as soon as members of these various nationalities or religious groups wrote *history*—ah, now, we had a different story (and of course a different history) from each individual.

When I say above that "apparently" it didn't matter in the physical sciences, or the "exact sciences" as they are so often called, the truth is that it does matter there also. Every individual scientist is limited in his ability to abstract data from Nature by the brainwashing he has received from his parents and in school. As the General Semanticist would say, each scientific researcher "trails his history" into every research project. Thus, a physicist with less educational or personal rigidity can solve a problem that was beyond the ability (to abstract) of another physicist.

In short, the observer always is, and always has to be a "me". . . . a specific person.

Accordingly, as *World of Null-A* opens, my hero—Gilbert Gosseyn—becomes aware that he is not who he thinks. He has a belief about himself that is false.

Now, consider—analogically, this is true of all of us. Only, we are so far gone into falseness, so acceptant of our limited role, that we never question it at all.

. . . To continue with the story of *World:* Not knowing who he is, nevertheless, my protagonist gradually becomes familiar with his "identity." Which essentially means that he abstracts significance from the events that occur and gives them power over him. Presently he begins to feel that the part of his identity that he has abstracted is the whole.

This is demonstrated in the second novel, *The Players of Null-A.* In this sequel story, Gilbert Gosseyn rejects all attempts at being someone else. Since he is not consciously abstracting in this area (of identity), he remains a pawn. For a person who is rigidly bound by identifications with what might be called the noise of the universe, the world is rich and colorful, not he. His identity seems to be something because it is recording this enormous number of impacts from the environment.

The sum total of Gosseyn's abstractions from the environment—this includes his proprioceptive perceptions of his own body—constitutes his memory.

Thus, I presented the thought in these stories that memory equals identity.

But I didn't say it. I dramatized it.

For example: a third of the way through *World,* Gosseyn is violently killed. But there he is again at the beginning of the next chapter, apparently the same person but in another body. Because he has the previous body's memories, he accepts that he is the same identity.

An inverted example: At the end of *Players,* the main

9

antagonist, who believes in a specific religion, kills his god. It is too deadly a reality for him to confront; so he has to forget it. But to forget something so all-embracing, he must forget everything he ever knew. He forgets who he is.

In short, no-memory equates with no-self.

When you read *World* and *Players*, you'll see how consistently this idea is adhered to and—now that it has been called to your attention—how precise is the development.

I cannot at the moment recall a novel written prior to *World of Null-A* that had a deeper meaning than that which showed on the surface. Science fiction often seems so complicated all by itself when written straightforwardly without innuendoes or subtle implications on more than one level, that it seems downright cruel of a writer to add an extra dimension that is hidden. A recent example of such a two-level science fiction novel is the first of that genre written by the British existentialist philosopher, Colin Wilson, titled *The Mind Parasites*. The protagonist of *Parasites* was one of the New Men—an existentialist, in short.

In *World,* we have the Null-A (non-Aristotelian) man, who thinks gradational scale, not black and white —without, however, becoming a rebel or a cynic, or a conspirator, in any current meaning of the term. A little bit of this in the Communist hierarchies, Asia and Africa in general, and our own Wall Street and Deep South, and in other either-or thinking areas . . . and we'd soon have a more progressive planet.

Science fiction writers have recently been greatly concerned with characterization in science fiction. A few writers in the field have even managed to convey that *their* science fiction has this priceless quality.

To set the record straight as to where I stand in this controversy—in the Null-A stories I characterize identity itself.

Of greater significance than any squabble between a writer and his critics . . . General Semantics continues to have a meaningful message for the world today.

Did you read in the newspapers at the time about S.I. Hayakawa's handling of the San Francisco State College riots of 1968-69? They were among the first, and the most serious—out of control and dangerous. The president of the college resigned. Hayakawa was appointed interim president. What did he do? Well, Professor Hayakawa is today's Mr. Null-A himself, the elected head of the International Society for General Semantics. He moved into that riot with the sure awareness that in such situations communication is the key. But you must communicate in relation to the rules that the other side is operating by.

The honest demands of the people with genuine grievances were instantly over-met on the basis of better-thought. But the conspirators don't even know today what hit them and why they lost their forward impetus.

Such also happens in the fable of Gilbert GoSANE in *The World of Null-A.*

A. E. VAN VOGT

I

Common sense, do what it will, cannot avoid being surprised occasionally. The object of science is to spare it this emotion and create mental habits which shall be in such close accord with the habits of the world as to secure that nothing shall be unexpected.

B. R.

The occupants of each floor of the hotel must as usual during the games form their own protective groups. . . ."

Gosseyn stared somberly out of the curving corner window of his hotel room. From its thirty-story vantage point, he could see the city of the Machine spread out below him. The day was bright and clear, and the span of his vision was tremendous. To his left, he could see a blue-black river sparkling with the waves whipped up by the late-afternoon breeze. To the north, the low mountains stood out sharply against the high backdrop of the blue sky.

That was the visible periphery. Within the confines of the mountains and the river, the buildings that he could see crowded along the broad streets. Mostly, they were homes with bright roofs that glinted among palms and semitropical trees. But here and there were other hotels, and more tall buildings not identifiable at first glance.

The Machine itself stood on the leveled crest of a mountain.

It was a scintillating, silvery shaft rearing up into the sky nearly five miles away. Its gardens, and the presidential mansion near by, were partially concealed behind trees. But Gosseyn felt no interest in the setting. The Machine itself overshadowed every other object in his field of vision.

The sight of it was immensely bracing. In spite of himself, in spite of his dark mood, Gosseyn experienced a sense of wonder. Here he was, at long last, to participate in the games of the Machine—the games which meant wealth and position for those who were partially successful, and *the* trip to Venus for the special group that won top honors.

For years he had wanted to come, but it had taken *her* death to make it possible. Everything, Gosseyn thought bleakly, had its price. In all his dreams of this day, he had never suspected that she would not be there beside him, competing herself for the great prizes. In those days, when they had planned and studied together, it was power and position that had shaped their hopes. Going to Venus neither Patricia nor he had been able to imagine, nor had they considered it. Now, for him alone, the power and wealth meant nothing. It was the remoteness, the unthinkableness, the mystery of Venus, with its promise of forgetfulness, that attracted. He felt himself aloof from the materialism of Earth. In a completely unreligious sense, he longed for spiritual surcease.

A knock on the door ended the thought. He opened it and looked at the boy who stood there. The boy said, "I've been sent, sir, to tell you that all the rest of the guests on this floor are in the sitting room."

Gosseyn felt blank. "So what?" he asked.

"They're discussing the protection of the people on this floor, sir, during the games."

"Oh!" said Gosseyn.

He was shocked that he had forgotten. The earlier announcement coming over the hotel communicators about such protection had intrigued him. But it had been hard to believe that the world's greatest city would be entirely without police or court protection during the period of the games. In outlying cities, in all other towns, villages, and communities, the continuity of law went on. Here, in the city of the Machine, for a month there would be no law except the negative defensive law of the groups.

"They asked me to tell you," the boy said, "that those

14

who don't come are not protected in any way during the period of the games."

"I'll be right there," smiled Gosseyn. "Tell them I'm a newcomer and forgot. And thank you."

He handed the boy a quarter and waved him off. He closed the door, fastened the three plasto windows, and put a tracer on his videophone. Then, carefully locking the door behind him, he went out along the hall.

As he entered the sitting room, he noticed a man from his own town, a store proprietor named Nordegg, standing near the door. Gosseyn nodded and smiled a greeting. The man glanced at him curiously, but did not return either the smile or the nod. Briefly, that seemed odd. The unusualness of it faded from Gosseyn's mind as he saw that others of the large group present were looking at him.

Bright, friendly eyes, curious, friendly faces with just a hint of calculation in them—that was the impression Gosseyn had. He suppressed a smile. Everybody was sizing up everybody else, striving to determine what chance his neighbors had of winning in the games. He saw that an old man at a desk beside the door was beckoning to him. Gosseyn walked over. The man said, "I've got to have your name and such for our book here."

"Gosseyn," said Gosseyn. "Gilbert Gosseyn, Cress Village, Florida, age thirty-four, height six feet one inch, weight one hundred eighty-five, no special distinguishing marks."

The old man smiled up at him, his eyes twinkling. "That's what you think," he said. "If your mind matches your appearance, you'll go far in the games." He finished, "I notice you didn't say you were married."

Gosseyn hesitated, thinking of a dead woman. "No," he said finally, quietly, "not married."

"Well, you're a smart-looking man. May the games prove you worthy of Venus, Mr. Gosseyn."

"Thanks," said Gosseyn.

As he turned to walk away, Nordegg, the other man from Cress Village, brushed past him and bent over the ledger on the desk. When Gosseyn looked back a minute later, Nordegg was talking with animation to the old man, who seemed to be protesting. Gosseyn watched them, puzzled, then forgot them as a small, jolly-looking man walked to an open space in the crowded room and held up his hand.

"Ladies and gentlemen," he began, "I would say that we should now begin our discussions. Everybody interested in group protection has had ample time to come here. And therefore, as soon as the challenging period is over, I will move that the doors be locked and we start.

"For the benefit," he went on, "of those new to the games who do not know what I mean by challenging period, I will explain the procedure. As you know, everybody here present will be required to repeat into the lie detector the information he or she gave to the doorkeeper. But before we begin with that, if you have any doubts about the legitimacy of anybody's presence, please state them now. You have the right to challenge anybody present. Please voice any suspicions you have, even though you possess no specific evidence. Remember, however, that the group meets every week and that challenges can be made at each meeting. But now, any challenges?"

"Yes," said a voice behind Gosseyn. "I challenge the presence here of a man calling himself Gilbert Gosseyn."

"Eh?" said Gosseyn. He whirled and stared incredulously at Nordegg.

The man looked at him steadily, then his gaze went out to the faces beyond Gosseyn. He said, "When Gosseyn first came in, he nodded to me as if he knew me, and so I went over to the book to find out his name, thinking it might recall him to me. To my amazement I heard him give his address as Cress Village, Florida, which is where I come from. Cress Village, ladies and gentlemen, is a rather famous little place, but it has a population of only three hundred. I own one of the three stores, and I know everybody, absolutely everybody, in the village and in the surrounding countryside. There is no person residing in or near Cress Village by the name of Gilbert Gosseyn."

For Gosseyn, the first tremendous shock had come and gone while Nordegg was still speaking. The after-feeling that came was that he was being made ridiculous in some obscure way. The larger accusation seemed otherwise quite meaningless.

He said, "This all seems very silly, Mr. Nordegg." He

paused. "That is your name, is it not?"

"That's right," Nordegg nodded, "though I'm wondering how you found it out."

"Your store in Cress Village," Gosseyn persisted, "stands at the end of a row of nine houses, where four roads come together."

"There is no doubt," said Nordegg, "that you have been through Cress Village, either personally or by means of a photograph."

The man's smugness irritated Gosseyn. He fought his anger as he said, "About a mile westward from your store is a rather curiously shaped house."

"'House,' he calls it!" said Nordegg. "The world-famous Florida home of the Hardie family."

"Hardie," said Gosseyn, "was the maiden name of my late wife. She died about a month ago. Patricia Hardie. Does that strike any chord in your memory?"

He saw that Nordegg was grinning gleefully at the intent faces surrounding them.

"Well, ladies and gentlemen, you can judge for yourselves. He says that Patricia Hardie was his wife. That's a marriage I think we would all have heard about if it had ever taken place. And as for her being the late Patricia Hardie, or Patricia Gosseyn, well"—he smiled—"all I can say is, I saw her yesterday morning, and she was very, very much alive, and looking extremely proud and beautiful on her favorite horse, a white Arabian."

It wasn't ridiculous any more. None of this fitted. Patricia didn't own a horse, white or colored. They had been poor, working their small fruit farm in the daytime, studying at night. Nor was Cress Village world-famous as the country home of the Hardies. The Hardies were nobodies. Who the devil were they supposed to be?

The question flashed by. With a simple clarity he saw the means that would end the deadlock.

"I can only suggest," he said, "that the lie detector will readily verify my statement."

But the lie detector said, "No, you are not Gilbert Gosseyn, nor have you ever been a resident of Cress Village. You are—" It stopped. The dozens of tiny electronic tubes in it flickered uncertainly.

"Yes, yes," urged the pudgy man. "Who is he?"

There was a long pause, then: "No knowledge about that is available in his mind," said the detector. "There is an aura of unique strength about him. But he himself seems to be unaware of his true identity. Under the circumstances, no identification is possible."

"And under the circumstances," said the pudgy man with finality, "I can only suggest an early visit to a psychiatrist, Mr. Gosseyn. Certainly you cannot remain here."

A minute later, Gosseyn was out in the corridor. A thought, a purpose, lay on his brain like a cake of ice. He reached his room and put through a call on the videophone. It took two minutes to make the connection with Cress Village. A strange woman's face came onto the plate. It was a rather severe face, but distinctive and young.

"I'm Miss Treechers, Miss Patricia Hardie's Florida secretary. What is it you wish to speak to Miss Hardie about?"

For a moment the existence of such a person as Miss Treechers was staggering. Then: "It's private," said Gosseyn, recovering. "And it's important that I speak to her personally. Please connect me at once."

He must have sounded or looked or acted authoritative. The young woman said hesitantly, "I'm not supposed to do this, but you can reach Miss Hardie at the palace of the Machine."

Gosseyn said explosively, "She's *here,* in the great city!"

He was not aware of hanging up. But suddenly the woman's face was gone. The video was dark. He was alone with his realization: Patricia was alive!

He had known, of course. His brain, educated in accepting things as they were, had already adjusted to the fact that a lie detector didn't lie. Sitting there, he felt strangely satiated with information. He had no impulse to call the palace, to talk to her, to see her. Tomorrow, of course, he would have to go there, but that seemed far away in space-time. He grew aware that someone was knocking loudly at his door. He opened it to four men, the foremost of whom, a tall young man, said, "I'm the assistant manager. Sorry, but you'll have to leave. We'll check

18

your baggage downstairs. During the policeless month, we can take no chances with suspicious individuals."

It took about twenty minutes for Gosseyn to be ejected from the hotel. Night was falling as he walked slowly along the almost deserted street.

II

The gifted . . . Aristotle . . . affected perhaps the largest number of people ever influenced by a single man . . . . Our tragedies began when the "intensional" biologist Aristotle took the lead over the "extensional" mathematical philosopher Plato, and formulated all the primitive identifications, subject-predictivism . . . into an imposing system, which for more than two thousand years we were not allowed to revise under penalty of persecution. . . . Because of this, his name has been used for the two-valued doctrines of Aristotelianism, and, conversely, the many-valued realities of modern science are given the name non-Aristotelianism. . . .

A.K.

It was too early for grave danger. The night, though already arrived, was but beginning. The prowlers and the gangs, the murderers and the thieves, who would soon emerge into the open, were still waiting for the deeper darkness. Gosseyn came to a sign that flashed on and off, repeating tantalizingly:

ROOMS FOR THE UNPROTECTED
$20 a night

Gosseyn hesitated. He couldn't afford that price for the full thirty days of the games, but it might do for a few nights. Reluctantly, he rejected the possibility. There were ugly stories connected with such places. He preferred to risk the night in the open.

He walked on. As the planetary darkness deepened, more and more lights flashed on in their automatic fashion. The city of the Machine glowed and sparkled. For miles and miles along one street he crossed, he could see two-lines of street lamps like shining sentinels striding in geometric progression toward a distant blaze point of illusory meeting. It was all suddenly depressing.

He was apparently suffering from semi-amnesia, and he must try to comprehend that in the largest sense of meaning. Only thus would he be able to free himself from the emotional effects of his condition. Gosseyn attempted to visualize the freeing as an *event* in the null-A interpretation. The event that was himself, as he was, his body and mind as a whole, amnesia and all, as of this moment on this day and in this city.

Behind that conscious integration were thousands of hours of personal training. Behind the training was the non-Aristotelian technique of automatic extensional thinking, the unique development of the twentieth century which, after four hundred years, had become the dynamic philosophy of the human race. "The map is not the territory. . . . The word is not the thing itself. . . ." The belief that he had been married did not make it fact. The hallucinations which his unconscious mind had inflicted on his nervous system had to be counteracted.

As always, it worked. Like water draining from an overturned basin, the doubts and fears spilled out of him. The weight of false grief, false because it had so obviously been imposed on his mind for someone else's purpose, lifted. He was free.

He started forward again. As he walked, his gaze darted from side to side, seeking to penetrate the shadows of doorways. Street corners he approached alertly, his hand on his gun. In spite of his caution, he did not see the girl who came racing from a side street until an instant before she bumped into him with a violence that unbalanced them both.

The swiftness of the happening did not prevent precautions. With his left arm, Gosseyn snatched at the young woman. He caught her body just below the shoulders, imprisoning both of her arms in a viselike grip. With his right hand, he drew his gun. All in an instant. There followed a longer moment while he fought to recover from the imbalance her speed and weight had imposed on them both. He succeeded. He straightened. He half carried, half dragged her into the shadowed archway of a door. As he reached its shelter, the girl began to wriggle and to moan softly. Gosseyn brought his gun hand up and put it, gun and all, over her mouth.

"Sh-sh!" he whispered. "I'm not going to hurt you."

She ceased wriggling. She stopped her whimpering. He allowed her to free her mouth. She said breathlessly, "They were right behind me. Two men. They must have seen you and run off."

Gosseyn considered that. Like all the happenings in spacetime, this one was packed with unseen and unseeable factors. A young woman, different from all the other young women in the universe, had come running in terror from a side street. Her terror was either real or it was assumed. Gosseyn's mind skipped the harmless possibility and fastened upon the probability that her appearance was a trick. He pictured a small group waiting around the corner, anxious to share in the spoils of a policeless city, yet not willing to take the risk of a direct assault. He felt coldly, unsympathetically suspicious. Because if she was harmless, what was she doing out alone on such a night? He muttered the question savagely.

"I'm unprotected," came the husky answer. "I lost my job last week because I wouldn't go out with the boss. And I had no savings. My landlady put me out this morning when I couldn't pay my rent."

Gosseyn said nothing. Her explanation was so feeble that he couldn't have spoken without effort. After a moment, he wasn't so sure. His own story wouldn't sound any too plausible if he should ever make the mistake of putting it into words. Before committing himself to the possibility that she was telling the truth, he tried one question. "There's absolutely no place you can go?"

"None," she said. And that was that. She was his charge for the duration of the games. He led her unresisting out onto the sidewalk, and, carefully avoiding the corner, into the road.

"We'll walk on the center white line," he said. "That way we can watch the corners better."

The road had its own dangers, but he decided not to mention them.

"Now, look," Gosseyn went on earnestly, "don't be afraid of me. I'm in a mess, too, but I'm honest. So far as

I am concerned, we're in the same predicament, and our only purpose right now is to find a place where we can spend the night."

She made a sound. To Gosseyn it seemed like a muffled laugh, but when he whirled on her, her face was averted from the nearest street light and he couldn't be sure. She turned a moment later to face him, and he had his first real look at her. She was young, with thin but heavily tanned cheeks. Her eyes were dark pools, her lips parted. She wore makeup, but it wasn't a good job and added nothing to her beauty. She didn't look as if she had laughed at anything or anybody for a long time. Gosseyn's suspicion faded. But he was aware that he was back where he had started, protector of a girl whose individuality had not yet shown itself in any tangible form.

The vacant lot, when they came opposite it, made Gosseyn pause thoughtfully. It was dark, and there was brush scattered over it. It was an ideal hiding place for marauders of the night. But, looked at from another angle, it was also a possible shelter for an honest man and his protégée, provided they could approach it without being seen. He noticed after a brief survey that there was a back alley leading to the rear of the vacant lot, and a space between two stores through which they could get to the alley.

It took ten minutes to locate a satisfactory patch of grass under a low, spreading shrub.

"We'll sleep here," Gosseyn whispered.

She sank down. And it was the wordlessness of her acquiescence that brought the sudden realization that she had come with him too easily. He lay thoughtful, eyes narrowed, pondering the possible dangers.

There was no moon, and the darkness under the overhanging bush was intense. After a while, a long while, Gosseyn could see the shadowlike figure of her in a splash of dim light reflections from a distant street lamp. She was more than five feet from him, and all those first minutes that he watched her she didn't move perceptibly. Studying the shadow shape of her, Gosseyn grew increasingly conscious of the unknown factor she represented. She was at least as unknown as he himself. His speculation ended as the young woman said softly, "My name is Teresa Clark. What's yours?"

What indeed? Gosseyn wondered. Before he could speak, the girl added, "Are you here for the games?"

"That's right," said Gosseyn.

He hesitated. It was he who ought to be asking the questions.

"And you?" he said. "Are you here for the games, too?"

It took a moment to realize that he had propounded a leading question. Her answer was bitter-voiced. "Don't be funny. I don't even know what null-A stands for."

Gosseyn was silent. There was a humility here that embarrassed him. The girl's personality was suddenly clearer: a twisted ego that would shortly reveal a complete satisfaction with itself. A car raced past on the near-by street, ending the need for comment. It was followed rapidly by four more. The night was briefly alive with the thrum of tires on pavement. The sound faded. But vague echoes remained, distant throbbing noises which must have been there all the time but which now that his attention had been aroused became apparent.

The young woman's voice intruded; she had a nice voice, though there was a plaintive note of self-pity in it that was not pleasant. "What is all this games stuff, anyway? In a way, it's easy enough to see what happens to winners who stay on Earth. They get all the juicy jobs; they become judges, governors, and such. But what about the thousands who every year win the right to go to Venus? What do they do when they get there?"

Gosseyn was noncommittal. "Personally," he said, "I think I'll be satisfied with the presidency."

The girl laughed. "You'll have to go some," she said, "to beat the Hardie gang."

Gosseyn sat up. "To beat *whom?*" he asked.

"Why, Michael Hardie, president of Earth."

Slowly, Gosseyn sank back to the ground. So that was what Nordegg and the others at the hotel had meant. His story must have sounded like the ravings of a lunatic. President Hardie, Patricia Hardie, a palatial summer home at Cress Village—and every bit of information in his brain about that absolutely untrue.

Who could have planted it there? The Hardies?

"Could you," came Teresa Clark's voice slowly, "teach

23

me how to win some minor job through the games?"

"What's that?" In the darkness Gosseyn stared at her. His astonishment yielded to a kindlier impulse. "I don't see how it could be done," he said. "The games require knowledge and skill integrated over a long period. During the last fifteen days, they require such flexibility of understanding that only the keenest and most highly developed brains in the world can hope to compete."

"I'm not interested in the last fifteen days. If you reach the seventh day, you get a job. That's right, isn't it?"

"The lowest job competed for in the games," Gosseyn explained gently, "pays ten thousand a year. The competition, I understand, is slightly terrific."

"I'm pretty quick," said Teresa Clark. "And I'm desperate. That should help."

Gosseyn doubted it, but he felt sorry for her.

"If you wish," he said, "I'll give you a very brief résumé."

He paused. She said quickly, "Please go on."

Gosseyn hesitated. He felt foolish again at the thought of talking to her on the subject. He began reluctantly, "The human brain is roughly divided into two sections, the cortex and the thalamus. The cortex is the center of discrimination, the thalamus the center of the emotional reactions of the nervous system." He broke off. "Ever been to the Semantics building?"

"It was wonderful," said Teresa Clark. "All those jewels and precious metals."

Gosseyn bit his lip. "I don't mean that. I mean the picture story on the walls. Did you see that?"

"I don't remember." She seemed to realize she was not pleasing him. "But I saw the bearded man—what's his name?—the director?"

"Lavoisseur?" Gosseyn frowned into the darkness. "I thought he was killed in an accident a few years ago. When did you see him?"

"Last year. He was in a wheel chair."

Gosseyn frowned. Just for a moment he had thought his memory was going to play him false again. It seemed odd, though, that whoever had tampered with his mind had not wanted him to know that the almost legendary Lavoisseur

24

was still alive. He hesitated, then returned to what he had been saying earlier.

"Both the cortex and the thalamus have wonderful potentialities. Both should be trained to the highest degree, but particularly they should be organized so that they will work in co-ordination. Wherever such co-ordination, or integration, does not occur, you have a tangled personality—over-emotionalism and, in fact, all variations of neuroticism. On the other hand, where cortical-thalamic integration has been established, the nervous system can withstand almost any shock."

Gosseyn stopped, recalling the shock his own brain had suffered a short time before. The girl said quickly, "What's the matter?"

"Nothing." Gruffly. "We can can talk about it again in the morning."

He was suddenly weary. He lay back. His last thought before he drifted into sleep was wonder as to what the lie detector had meant when it said, "There is an aura of unique strength about him."

When he wakened, the sun was shining. Of Teresa Clark there was no sign.

Gosseyn verified her absence by a quick search through the brush. Then he walked to the sidewalk a hundred feet away, and glanced along the street, first north, then south.

The sidewalks and the road were alive with traffic. Men and women, gaily dressed, hurried along past where Gosseyn stood. The sound of many voices and many machines made a buzz and a roar and a hum. It was suddenly exciting. To Gosseyn there came exhilaration and, stronger now, the realization that he was free. Even the girl's departure proved that she was not the second step in some fantastic plan that had begun with the attack on his memory. It was a relief to have her off his hands.

A familiar face detached itself from the human countenances that had been flashing past him. Teresa Clark, carrying two brown paper bags, hailed him.

"I've brought some breakfast," she said. "I thought you'd prefer to picnic out among the ants, rather than try to get into a packed restaurant."

They ate in silence. Gosseyn noted that the food she

25

had brought had been daintily put up in boxes and plasto containers for outside service. There was reinforced orange juice, cereal, with cream in a separate plasto, hot kidneys on toast, and coffee, also with its separate cream.

Five dollars, he estimated. Which was pure luxury for a couple who had to live for thirty days on a very small amount of money. And, besides, a girl who possessed five dollars would surely have paid it to her landlady for another night's lodging. Furthermore, she must have had a good job to think in terms of such a breakfast. That brought a new thought. Gosseyn frowned over it a moment, then said, "This boss of yours who made the passes at you—what's his name?"

"Huh?" said Teresa Clark. She had finished her kidneys and was searching for her purse. Now she looked up, startled. Then her face cleared. "Oh, him!" she said.

There was a pause.

"Yes," Gosseyn urged. "What's his name?"

She was completely recovered. "I'd prefer to forget about him," said Teresa Clark. "It's not pleasant." She changed the subject. "Will I have to know much for the first day?"

Gosseyn hesitated, half inclined to pursue further the subject of her boss. He decided not to. He said, "No. Fortunately, the first day has never been more than a perfunctory affair. It consists primarily of registrations and of being assigned to the cubbyhole where you take your early tests. I've studied the published records of the games of the last twenty years, which is the furthest back the Machine'll ever release, and I've noticed that there is never any change in the first day. You are required to define what null-A, null-N, and null-E stand for.

"Whether you realize it or not, you cannot have lived on Earth without picking up some of the essence of null-A. It's been a growing part of our common mental environment for several hundred years." He finished, "People, of course, have a tendency to forget definitions, but if you're really in earnest about this—"

"You bet I am," said the girl.

She drew a cigarette case out of her purse. "Have a cigarette."

The cigarette case glittered in the sun. Diamonds,

26

emeralds, and rubies sparkled on its intricately wrought gold surface. A cigarette, already lighted in some automatic fashion inside the case, protruded from its projector. The gems could have been plastic, the gold imitation. But it looked handmade, and its apparent genuineness was staggering. Gosseyn put its value at twenty-five thousand`dollars.

He found his voice. "No, thanks," he said. "I don't smoke."

"It's a special brand," said the young woman insistently. "Deliciously mild."

Gosseyn shook his head. And this time she accepted the refusal. She removed the cigarette from the case, put it to her lips, and inhaled with a deep satisfaction, then plunged the case back into her purse. She seemed unconscious of the sensation it had caused. She said, "Let's get busy with my studies. Then we can separate and meet here again tonight. Is that all right?"

She was a very dominating young woman, and Gosseyn wasn't sure that he could even learn to like her. His suspicion that she had come into his life with a purpose was stronger. She was possibly a connecting link between himself and whoever had tampered with his brain. He couldn't let her get away.

"All right," he said. "But there isn't any time to waste."

III

To be is to be related.

C.J.K.

Gosseyn helped the girl off the surface car. They walked rapidly around a screening nest of trees, through massive gates, and came in sight of the Machine. The girl walked unconcernedly on. But Gosseyn stopped.

The Machine was at the far end of a broad avenue. Mountaintops had been leveled so that it could have space and gardens around it. It was a full half mile from the tree-sheltered gates. It reared up and up in a shining metal splendor. It was a cone pointing into the lower heavens and crowned by a star of atomic light, brighter than the noonday sun above.

The sight of it so near shocked Gosseyn. He hadn't thought of it before, but he realized suddenly that the Machine would never accept his false identity. He felt a constriction, and stood there shaken and depressed. He saw that Teresa Clark had paused and was looking back at him.

"This is your first time to see it close?" she said sympathetically. "It does get you, doesn't it?"

There was a hint of superiority in her manner that brought a wan smile to Gosseyn's lips. These city slickers! he thought wryly. He felt better and, taking her arm, started forward again. His confidence grew slowly. Surely the Machine would not judge him on such a high abstraction as nominal identity, when even the lie detector in the hotel had recognized that he was not purposely misrepresenting himself.

The crowds became unwieldy as they approached the base of the Machine, and the bigness of the Machine itself was more apparent. Its roundness and its size gave a sleek, streamlined appearance that was not canceled by the tiers of individual game rooms which ornamented and broke up its gigantic base. Right around the base the rooms extended. The entire first floor consisted of game rooms and corridors leading to them. Broad outside staircases led to the second, third, and fourth floors and down into three basements, a total of seven floors entirely devoted to game rooms for individual competitors.

"Now that I'm here," said Teresa Clark, "I'm no longer so sure of myself. These people look darned intelligent."

Gosseyn laughed at the expression on her face, but he said nothing. He felt supremely positive that he could compete right through to the thirtieth day. His problem was not would he win, but would he be allowed to try.

Aloof and impregnable, the Machine towered above the human beings it was about to sort according to their semantic training. No one now living knew exactly in what part of its structure its electron-magnetic brain was located. Like many men before him, Gosseyn speculated about that. "Where would I have put it?" he wondered, "if I had been one of the scientist-architects?" It didn't matter, of course. The Machine was already older than any known living human being. Self-renewing, conscious of its life and of its purpose, it remained greater than any individual, immune to bribery and corruption and theoretically capable of preventing its own destruction.

"Juggernaut!" emotional men had screamed when it was being built. "No," said the builders, "not a destroyer, but an immobile, mechanical brain with creative functions and a capacity to add to itself in certain sane directions." In three hundred years, people had come to accept its decisions as to who should rule them.

Gosseyn grew aware of a conversation between a man and a woman who were walking near by.

"It's the policeless part," the woman was saying. "It frightens me."

The man said, "Don't you see, that shows what Venus must be like, where no police are necessary. If we prove worthy of Venus, we go to a planet where everyone is sane. The policeless period gives us a chance to measure progress down here. At one time it was a nightmare, but I've noticed a change even in my lifetime. It's necessary, all right."

"I guess here's where we separate," said Teresa Clark. "The C's are down on the second basement, the G's just above them. Meet me tonight at the vacant lot. Any objections?"

"None."

Gosseyn waited till she was out of sight down a stairway that led to the second basement. Then he followed. He caught a glimpse of her as he reached the bottom of the steps. She was pushing toward an exit at the end of a far corridor. He was halfway along the corridor when she ran up a staircase that led outside. By the time Gosseyn shoved his way up the stairs, she was nowhere to be seen. He turned back thoughtfully. The possibility that she would not risk the tests had made him follow her, but it was disturbing to have his suspicions proved. The problem of Teresa Clark was becoming more complex.

More upset than he had expected, Gosseyn entered a vacant examination booth in the G section. The door had barely clicked shut behind him when a voice from a speaker said matter of factly, "Your name?"

Gosseyn forgot Teresa Clark. Here was the crisis.

The booth contained a comfortable swivel chair, a desk with drawers, and a transparent paneling above the desk, behind which electron tubes gleamed in a variety of cherry-red and flame-yellow patterns. In the center of the panels, also made of transparent plastic, was an ordinary streamlined speaker. It was from this that the voice of the Machine had come. It repeated now, "Your name? And please grasp the nodes."

"Gilbert Gosseyn," said Gosseyn quietly.

There was silence. Some of the cherry-red tubes flickered unsteadily. Then: "For the time being," said the Machine in a casual tone, "I'll accept that name."

Gosseyn sank back deeper into the chair. His skin warmed with excitement. He felt himself on the verge of discovery. He said, "You know my true name?"

There was another pause. Gosseyn had time to think of a machine that was at this very moment conducting *tens of thousands* of easygoing conversations with the individuals in every cubbyhole in its base. Then: "No record in your mind of another name," said the Machine. "But let's leave that for now. Ready for your test?"

"B-but—"

"No further questions at this moment," said the Machine more formally. Its tone was comfortable when it spoke again. "You'll find writing materials in one of the drawers. The questions are printed on each sheet. Take your time. You've got thirty minutes, and you won't be able to leave the room till they're up. Good luck."

The questions were as Gosseyn had expected: "What is non-Aristotelianism? What is non-Newtonianism? What is non-Euclidianism?"

The questions were not really easy. The best method was not to attempt a detailed reply but to show consciousness of the multi-ordinal meaning of words, and of the fact that every answer could be only an abstraction. Gosseyn began by putting down the recognized abbreviation for each term—null-A, null-N, and null-E.

He finished in about twenty minutes, then sat back tingling with anticipation. The Machine had said, "No further questions at this moment." That seemed to imply that it would talk to him again. At the end of twenty-five minutes its voice came once more.

"Please don't be surprised at the simplicity of today's test. Remember, the purpose of the games is not to beguile the great majority of the contestants into losing. The purpose is to educate every individual of the race to make the best possible use of the complex nervous system which he or she has inherited. That can only be realized when everybody survives the full thirty days of the games. And now, those who failed today's test have already been informed. They will not be accepted as contestants during the rest of this season's games. To the rest—more than ninety-nine per cent, I am happy to say—good luck for tomorrow."

It was fast work. He had simply put his paper into the slot provided. A television tube had scanned it, compared it to the correct answers in highly flexible fashion, and recorded a pass. The answers of the twenty-five thousand other contestants had been similarly judged. In a few minutes another group of contestants would repeat the experience.

"You wish to ask more questions, Gilbert Gosseyn?" asked the Machine.

Gosseyn tensed. "Yes. I have had some false ideas planted in my mind. Were they put there with a purpose?"

"They were."

"Who put them there?"

"No records of that exists in your brain."

"Then how do you know they were put there?"

"Logical reasoning," said the Machine, "on the basis of information. The fact that your illusion was related to Patricia Hardie is very suggestive to me."

Gosseyn hesitated, then spoke the thought that had been in his mind. "Many psychoneurotics have equally strong beliefs. Such people usually claim identification with the great: 'I am Napoleon'; 'I am Hitler'; 'I am Tharg'; 'I am married to Patricia Hardie.' Was my false belief in that category?"

"Definitely no. Very strong convictions can be induced by hypnotic means. Yours comes under that heading. That is why you were able to throw off the emotion of grief when you first learned that she was not dead. Your recovery is not yet completed, however."

There was a pause. Then the Machine spoke again and there was a curious sadness in its words. "I am only an immobile brain, but dimly aware of what is transpiring in remote parts of Earth. What plans are brewing I can only guess. You will be surprised and disappointed to learn that I can tell you nothing more about that."

"What can you tell me?" asked Gosseyn.

"That you are very deeply involved, but that I cannot solve your problem. I want you to go to a psychiatrist and have a photograph taken of your cortex. I have an impression of something in your brain, but I cannot define it. And now that is all I will say to you. Good-by until tomorrow."

There was a click from the door as it unlocked automatically. Gosseyn went out into the corridor, hesitated for a moment, and then worked his way northward through the hurrying crowds.

He found himself on a paved boulevard. To the northwest, starting at about a quarter of a mile from the Machine, other buildings began. They were geometrically arranged in clusters around the boulevard, at the far end of which, amid embanked flowers and trees, stood the palace of the Machine.

The palace was not tall; its stately contours nestled among the vivid green and brilliance of its verdant environment. But that wasn't what held Gosseyn. His mind was reaching, visualizing, comprehending. President Hardie and his daughter Patricia lived there. If he was deeply involved, then so must they be. What had made them plant in his mind the conviction that he was married to a *dead* Patricia? It seemed futile. Any hotel-group lie detector would have found him out even if Nordegg hadn't been around to accuse him.

Gosseyn turned and strode around the base of the Machine back toward the city proper. He ate lunch in a small restaurant near the river, then began to thumb through the yellow pages of a telephone directory. He knew the name he was looking for, and he found it almost right away:

ENRIGHT, DAVID LESTER, psychologist
709 Medical Arts Building

Enright had written several books which were pre-scribed reading for anyone who hoped to get beyond the tenth day in the games. It was a pleasure to remember the crystal-like clarity of the man's writing, the careful semantic consideration given to every multi-ordinal word used, the breadth of intellect and understanding of the human body-and-mind-as-a-whole.

Gosseyn closed the directory and went out into the street. He felt at ease; his nerves were calm. Hope was surging in him. The very fact that he remembered Enright and his books in such detail showed how lightly the in-truding amnesia rested on his memory. It shouldn't take long once the famous man began to work on him. The reception clerk in the doctor's office said, "Dr. Enright can be seen by appointment only. I can give you an hour three days from now; that is, Thursday at two P.M. You must, however, make a twenty-five-dollar deposit."

Gosseyn paid the money, accepted his receipt, and went out. He was disappointed, but not too much so. Good doc-tors were bound to be busy men in a world that was still far from having attained null-A perfection.

On the street again, he watched one of the longest, most powerful cars he had ever seen slide past him and draw up at the curb a hundred feet away. The car gleamed in the afternoon sun. A liveried attendant leaped smartly from beside the driver and opened the door.

Teresa Clark stepped out. She wore an afternoon dress of some dark, rich material. The ensemble did not make her appear less slim, but the dark coloring of the dress made her face seem a little fuller and, by contrast, not so heavily tanned. Teresa Clark! The name was meaningless in the face of this magnificence.

"Who," Gosseyn asked a man who had stopped beside him, "is that?"

The stranger glanced at him in surprise and then he spoke the name Gosseyn had already guessed. "Why, that's Patricia Hardie, daughter of President Hardie. Quite a neurotic, I understand. Look at that car, for instance. Like an oversize jewel, a sure sign of—"

Gosseyn was turning away, turning his face from the car and its recent occupant. No sense in being recognized until he had thought this through. It seemed ridiculous that she would actually come again that very night to a dark lot to be alone with a strange man.

But she was there.

Gosseyn stood in the shadows staring thoughtfully at the shadow figure of the girl. He had come to the rendezvous very skillfully. Her back was to him and she seemed to be unaware of his presence. It was possible, in spite of his careful reconnoitering of the entire block, that he was already in a trap. But it was a risk he felt no hesitation in taking. Here, in this girl, was the only clue he had to the mystery of himself. He watched her curiously as well as he could in the developing darkness.

She was sitting, in the beginning, with her left foot tucked under her right leg. In the course of ten minutes, she changed her position five times. Twice during the shifts, she half stood up. In between, she spent some time apparently tracing figures on the grass with her finger. She pulled out her cigarette case and put it away again without taking a cigarette. She jerked her head half a dozen times, as if in defiance of some thought. She shrugged her shoulders twice, folded her arms and shivered as if with a chill, sighed audibly three times, clicked her tongue impatiently, and for about one whole minute she sat intensely still.

She hadn't been so nervous the night before. She hadn't, except for the little period when she was acting fearful of the men who were supposed to have been chasing her, seemed nervous at all. It was the waiting, Gosseyn decided. She was geared to meeting people, and to handling them. Alone, she had no resources of patience.

What was it the man had said that afternoon? Neurotic. There was no doubt of it. As a child she must have been denied that early null-A training so necessary to the development of certain intelligences. Just how such training could have been neglected in the home of a superbly integrated man such as President Hardie was a puzzle. Whatever the reason, she was one human being whose thalamus was always in full control of her actions. He could imagine her having a nervous breakdown.

He continued to watch her there in that almost darkness. After ten minutes, she stood up and stretched, then she sat down again. She took off her shoes, and, rolling over toward Gosseyn, lay down on the grass. She saw Gosseyn.

"It's all right," Gosseyn assured her softly. "It's only me. I guess you heard me coming."

He guessed nothing of the kind, but she had jerked to a sitting position, and it seemed the best way to soothe her.

"You gave me a start," she said. But her voice was calm and unstartled, properly subdued. She had suave thalamic reactions, this girl.

He sank down on the grass near her and let the feel of the night creep upon him. The second policeless night! It seemed hard to believe. He could hear the noises of the city, faint, unexciting, quite unsuggestive. Where were the gangs and the thieves? They seemed unreal, examined from the safety of this dark hiding place. Perhaps the years and the great educational system had winnowed their numbers, leaving only the fearful legend and a few wretches who slunk through the night seeking the helpless. No, that couldn't be right. Men were becoming more brave, not less, as their minds grew progressively integrated with the structure of the universe around them. Somewhere violence was being planned or performed. Somewhere? Perhaps here.

Gosseyn looked at the girl. Then very softly he began to talk. He described his plight—the way he had been kicked out of the hotel, the amnesia that hid his memory, the curious delusion that he had been married to Patricia Hardie. "And then," he finished ruefully, "she turned out to be the daughter of the president and very much alive."

Patricia Hardie said, "These psychologists, such as the one you're going to—is it true that they're all people who have won the trip to Venus in the games, and have come back to Earth to practice their profession? And that actually no one else can go in for psychiatry and the related sciences?"

Gosseyn hadn't thought of that. "Why, yes," he said. "Others can train for it of course, but—"

He was conscious of a sudden eagerness, a desire for the moment of the interview with Doctor Enright to arrive. How much he might learn from such a man! Caution came then, wonder as to why she had asked *that* question

35

instead of commenting on his story as a whole. In the dark he stared at her searchingly. But her face, her expression, was nightwrapped. Her voice came again.

"You mean, you haven't the faintest idea who you are? How did you get to the hotel in the first place?"

Gosseyn said soberly, "I have a memory of taking a bus from Cress Village to the airport at Nolendia. And I distinctly remember being on the plane."

"Did you have any meals aboard?"

Gosseyn took his time remembering. It was an intensional world into which he strove to penetrate and as nonexistent as all such worlds. Memory never was the thing remembered, but at least with most people, when there was a memory, there normally *had* been a fact of similar structure. His mind held nothing that could be related to physical structure. He hadn't eaten, definitely and unequivocally.

The girl was speaking. "You really haven't the faintest idea what this is all about? You have no purpose, no plan for dealing with it? You're just moving along in a great dark?"

Gosseyn said, "That's right." And waited.

The silence was long. Too long. And the answer, when it came, did not come from the girl. Somebody jumped on him and held him down. Other figures swarmed out of the brush and grabbed at him. He was on his feet, shoving at the first man. A tight horror made him fight even after a tangle of strong hands held him beyond his capacity to escape.

A man said, "O.K. Put 'em in the cars and let's get out of here."

As he was bundled into the back seat of a roomy sedan, Gosseyn thought, Had these people come in response to a signal from the girl? Or were they a gang?

A violent forward jerk of the car ended temporarily his tense speculation.

IV

Science is nothing but good sense and sound reasoning.
Stanislaus Leszcynski,
King of Poland, 1763

As the cars raced north along deserted streets, Gosseyn saw that there were two ahead of him and three behind. He could see their black, moving shapes through the windshield and in the rear-view mirror. Patricia Hardie was in one of them, but in spite of straining his eyes he could not make her out. Not that it mattered. He had looked over his captors and the suspicion that this was not a street gang was sharper now.

He spoke to the man who sat at his right. No answer. He turned to the man at his left. Before Gosseyn could speak, the man said, "We are not authorized to talk to you."

"Authorized!" Street gangsters didn't talk like that. Gosseyn sank back into his seat considerably relieved. The cars finally made a great curve and swooped into a tunnel. Minute by minute they raced forward on an upward slant through a dimly lighted cavern. After about five minutes, the tunnel ahead grew lighter. Abruptly the cars emerged into a circular, streamlined court. They slowed and then drew up before a doorway.

Men began to climb out of them. Gosseyn had a glimpse of the girl as she emerged from the car ahead of his. She came back and peered in at him.

"Just to keep the record straight," she said, "I'm Patricia Hardie."

"Yes," said Gosseyn, "I've known since this afternoon. Somebody pointed you out to me."

Her eyes grew brighter. "You damned fool," she said, "why didn't you beat it?"

"Because I've got to know. I've got to know about myself."

There must have been a tone in his voice, something of the empty feeling of a man who had lost his identity.

"You poor idiot," said Patricia Hardie in a softer voice.

"Just now, when they're nerving themselves for the plunge, they have spies in every hotel. What the lie detector said about you was reported at once. And they simply won't take any chances."

She hesitated. "Your hope," she said drably, "is that Thorson remains uninterested. My father is trying to persuade him to examine you, but so far he regards you as unimportant."

Once more she paused, then, "I'm sorry," she said, and turned away. She did not look back. She walked off toward a distant door that opened before her touch. Momentarily it revealed a very bright anteroom, then the door closed. Anywhere from five to ten minutes went by. Finally, a hawk-nosed man sauntered over from another door, and looked in at Gosseyn. He said, with an unmistakable sneer, "So this is the dangerous man!"

It seemed a futile insult. Gosseyn started to carry on with his examination of the man's physical characteristics, and then the import of the words penetrated. He had been expecting to be asked to get out of the car. Now he settled back in his seat. The idea that he was considered a dangerous man was absolutely new. It didn't seem to have any structural relation to the facts. Gilbert Gosseyn was a trained null-A whose brain had been damaged by an amnesic calamity. He might prove worthy of Venus in the games, but he would simply be one of thousands of similarly successful contenders. He had yet to show a single quality of structural difference between himself and other human beings.

"Ah, silence," drawled the big man. "The null-A pause, I suppose. Any moment now, your present predicament will have been integrated into control of your cortex, and semantically clever words will sound forth."

Gosseyn studied the man curiously. The sneer on the other's lips had relaxed. His expression was less cruel, his manner not so animalistically formidable. Gosseyn said pityingly, "I can only assume that you're a man who has failed at the games and that is why you are sneering at them. You poor fool!"

The big man laughed. "Come along," he said. "You've got some shocks coming. My name, by the by, is Thorson—Jim Thorson. I can tell you that without fear of its going any further."

"Thorson!" Gosseyn echoed, and then he was silent. Without another word, he followed the hawk-nosed man through an ornate door and into the palace of the Machine, where President and Patricia Hardie lived.

He began to think of the necessity of making a determined effort to escape. But not yet. Funny, to feel that so strongly. To know that learning about himself was more important than anything else.

There was a long marble corridor that ended in an open oak door. Thorson held the door for Gosseyn, a smile twisting his long face. Then he came in and closed the door behind him, shutting out the guards who had been following Gosseyn.

Three people were waiting in the room, Patricia Hardie and two men. Of the latter, one was a fine-looking chap of about forty-five, who sat behind a desk. But it was the second man who snatched Gosseyn's attention.

He had been in an accident. He was a patched monstrosity. He had a plastic arm and a plastic leg, and his back was in a plastic cage. His head looked as if it were made of opaque glass; it was earless. Two human eyes peered from under a glass-smooth dome of surgical plastic. He had been lucky in a limited fashion. From his eyes down, the lower part of his face was intact. He had a face. His nose, mouth, chin, and neck were human. Beyond that, his resemblance to anything normal depended partly upon the mental concessions of the observer. For the moment, Gosseyn was not prepared to make any concessions. He had decided on a course of action, a level of abstraction—boldness. He said, "What the devil is that?"

The creature chuckled in a bass amusement. His voice, when he spoke, was deep as a viol's G string.

"Let us," he said, "consider me as the 'X' quantity."

Gosseyn glanced away from "X" to the girl. Her gaze held his coolly, though a shade of heightened color crept into her cheeks. She had made a quick change into another dress, an evening gown. It gave a tone to her appearance that Teresa Clark had never had.

It was curiously hard to turn his attention to the other man. Even to his trained brain, the reorientation necessary to acceptance of President Hardie of Earth as a plotter was a hurdle too big for easy surmounting. But in the end there could be no shrinking from the identification.

Illegal actions were being taken. People didn't do what had been done to him, or say what Patricia and Thorson had said, unless it meant something. Even the Machine had hinted of imminent unpleasantness. And it had practically said in so many words that the Hardie family was involved.

The President, seen at this near distance, had the hard eyes of the disciplinarian and the smile of a man who must be tactful and pleasant to many people. His lips were thin. He looked as if he could cut an interview short or keep it firmly to the point. The man looked like an executive, alert, accustomed to the exercise of authority. He said now, "Gosseyn, we are men who would have been doomed to minor positions if we had accepted the rule of the Machine and the philosophy of null-A. We are highly intelligent and capable in every respect, but we have certain ruthless qualities in our natures that would normally bar us from great success. Ninety-nine per cent of the world's history was made by our kind, and you may be sure it shall be so again."

Gosseyn stared at him, a tightness gathering over his heart. He was being told too much. Either the plot was about to come into the open, or the vague threats that had already been leveled at him had the deadliest meanings. Hardie was continuing.

"I have told you this in order to emphasize the following instructions: Gosseyn, there are several guns pointing at you. You will accordingly without fuss walk over to that chair"—he motioned with his right hand—"and you will submit to manacles and other such minor indignities."

His gaze traveled beyond Gosseyn. He said, "Thorson, bring over the necessary machines."

Gosseyn knew better than to hope to escape from this room. He walked forward and allowed Thorson to handcuff his wrists to the arms of the chair. He watched with tense curiosity as the big man wheeled over a table with a number of small, delicate-looking machines on it.

Silently, Thorson attached a dozen cup-shaped devices on one of the machines to Gosseyn's skin with adhesive—six of them to his head and face, the other six to his throat, shoulders, and the upper part of his back.

Gosseyn grew aware that he was not the only over-wrought person in the room. The two men, Hardie and the monstrosity, leaned forward in their chairs. Blue eyes and yellow-brown eyes glowed moistly avid. The girl sat crouched in her chair, her legs drawn up, one hand rigidly holding a cigarette to her lips. She puffed at it automatically, but she didn't inhale. She simply puffed the smoke into her mouth and then thrust it out again. She did that over and over.

Of the quartet, Thorson was the calmest. With steady fingers, he made some final adjustments on something in the machine that Gosseyn couldn't see, then looked questioningly at Michael Hardie. But it was Gosseyn who broke the silence, who said thickly, "I think you ought to listen to me for a moment."

He paused, not because he was finished but because suddenly he felt desperate. He thought, What in the name of reason is going on here? This can't be happening to a law-abiding human being on the peaceful Earth of 2560 A.D.

"I feel," he said, and his voice sounded husky in his own ears, "like a child in a madhouse. You want something from me. For logic's sake, tell me what, and I'll do my best for you.

"Naturally," he went on, "I value my life more than any fact that you can possibly require of me. I can say that safely because in this world of null-A no individual matters to the extent that his ideas, his inventions, or his personality can be used to the detriment of mankind. Individual machines cannot sway the balance against the accumulated mass of science as employed by determined, courageous men in the defense of civilization. That has been proved. Unique science cannot win a war." He gazed questioningly at Michael Hardie. "Is it anything like that? Any invention of my pre-amnesic days?"

"No." The speaker was "X." The cripple looked amused, and added, "You know, this is really interesting. Here is a man who knows neither his purpose nor his antecedents, and yet his appearance at this period cannot be quite accidental. The inability of the hotel lie detector to penetrate his true identity is an unheard-of phenomenon."

"But he's telling the truth." Patricia Hardie lowered her feet to the floor, and let her cigarette hand dangle. She looked and sounded very earnest. "The lie detector at the hotel said that his mind was not aware of his identity."

A plastic arm waved at her patronizingly. The bass voice was tolerant.

"My dear young lady, I'm not questioning that it said that. But I'm not forgetting that machines are corruptible. The brilliant Mr. Crang, and I"—his voice grew significant—"have proved that to the satisfaction of many men, including your father."

He broke off. "I don't think any statement Gosseyn makes, or that is made about him by ordinary brain-testing devices, can be accepted by us."

President Hardie nodded. "He's right, Pat. Normally a man who falsely believed himself married to my daughter would be simply another psychoneurotic. However, the very appearance of such a man at *this* time would have to be investigated. But the inability of the hotel lie detector to identify him is so unnormal that, as you see"—he motioned—"even Thorson has become interested. My idea is that the Galactic League agents tossed him out for us to look at. Well, we're going to look. What are your plans, Jim?"

Thorson shrugged. "I want to break through the memory blocks and find out who he is."

"X" said, "I don't think that the information we gain should be too widely known. Miss Hardie, leave the room."

The girls lips tightened. "I prefer to stay," she said. She tossed her head defiantly. "After all, I took risks."

Nobody said anything. The half-man looked at her with eyes that, to Gosseyn, seemed implacable. Patricia Hardie stirred uneasily, then looked at her father as if for support. The great man evaded her gaze, twisting uncomfortably in his chair.

She got up, her lip curling. "So he's got you buffaloed, too," she said with a sneer. "Well, don't think he scares me. I'll put a bullet into him one of these days that no

42

surgeon will be able to put a plasto over."

She went out, slamming the door behind her. Hardie said, "I don't believe we need waste any time."

There were no objections. Gosseyn saw that Thorson's fingers were hovering over the power switch of the machine on the table. The moving fingers twisted powerfully. There was a click and a hum.

At first nothing happened. He was tensed to resist energy flows. And there weren't any. Blankly he watched the machine. It hummed and throbbed. Like so many devices, it had its own special electron tubes. Whether they were used for controlling the speed of unseen motors or for amplifying some obscure sound in his body or converting energy or timing changes in an invisible process, or for any one of a hundred other tasks, it was impossible for Gosseyn to decide.

Some of the tubes peeped brightly out of holes in an opaque, curving plastic instrument box. Others, he knew, were too sensitive to be exposed to anything so violent as the normal temperature and brightness of a room. They would be hidden deep in their little enclosures with only a minute fraction of their easily irritated glass-smooth forms connected with the outside.

Watching hurt his eyes. He kept blinking and the tears that resulted blurred his vision. With an effort, Gosseyn looked away from the table and its machines. The movement must have been too sudden for his strained nerves. Something banged inside his head and a violent headache began. He realized with a start that this was what the machine was doing to him.

It was as if he had sunk to the bottom of a pool of water. There seemed to be heavy pressure on him from every side, *inside* included. As from a great distance, he heard Thorson's calm voice lecturing his hearers.

"This is an interesting machine. It manufactures a variation of nervous energy. The energy is absorbed through the dozen nodes I have placed on Gosseyn's head and shoulders, and flows evenly along all the nerve paths that have been previously established in his body. It does not itself establish any new patterns. You must think of it as an impulse that rejects instantly the slightest difficulty. It recoils from obstacles that vary by approximately one

43

per cent from what to it is normal. It is a supreme adherent of the school of energies that follow the path of least resistance."

It was hard, thinking against the sound of the voice. Gosseyn's mind couldn't form a complete thought. He strained against the blurring power of the voice and against the energy that was flowing through him. Nothing came but spasms of ideas and Thorson's voice.

"The medically interesting characteristic of this artifical flow of nervous energy is that it is photographable. In a few moments, as soon as the movement of artificial energy has penetrated the remotest easy paths, I'll obtain several negatives and make some positive prints. When enlarged in segments through a projector, the prints will show us in what parts of his brain his memory is concentrated. Since science has long known the nature of the memory stored in every cell group, we can then decide where to concentrate the pressures that will force the particular memory we want onto the verbal level.

"A further use of this machine, using more power and combined with a complicated word-association system-formula, will perform the actual operation." He shut off the machine and pulled some film out of the camera. He said, "Watch him!" He disappeared through the nearest door.

Watching wasn't necessary. Gosseyn couldn't have stood steadily on his feet. His brain was turning rapidly in an illusion of spinning. Like a child that has whirled around and around too often, he had to unwind. Thorson was back before he could see straight.

He entered slowly, and, ignoring both "X" and Hardie, walked over to Gosseyn. He had two prints in his hand, and he paused with them directly in front of his prisoner and stared at him.

"What have you found?" said Hardie from Gosseyn's left.

Thorson waved at him, an impatient command to be silent. It was a startlingly discourteous gesture and, what was more, he seemed to be unaware that he had made it. He stood there, and suddenly his personality was not just that of one more individual. *He had been holding it in.* Underneath the cold exterior was a blaze of nervous

44

energy, a supremely potent human being. Gosseyn saw that his manner was not one of the deference to superiors. It was command, assured, final, unequivocal. When he agreed with the others, it was because he wanted to. When he disagreed, *his* way was decisive.

"X" wheeled over and gently removed the prints from Thorson's fingers. He handed one to Hardie. The two men examined the photographs with two distinct and separate emotions.

"X" half climbed out of his chair. The movement revealed several things about his semi-plastic body. It showed his height. He was taller than Gosseyn had thought, at least five feet ten or eleven. It showed how his plastic arm was fastened to the plastic cage around the middle of his body. It showed that his face could look startled. He half whispered, "It's a good thing we didn't let him go to see that psychiatrist. We struck at the right moment, at the beginning."

Michael Hardie looked irritated. "What are you babbling about? Don't forget that I'm in my present position entirely because of your ability to control the games of the Machine. I never could get all this null-A stuff about the human brain into my head. All I see is a solid core of brightness. I presume that those are the lines of nerve patterns, and that they will untangle when enlarged on a screen."

This time Thorson heard. He walked over, pointed at something on the print, and whispered an explanation that slowly drained the color from Hardie's face.

"We'll have to kill him," he said grayly. "At once."

Thorson shook his head irritably. "Whatever for? What can he do? Warn the world?" He grew more intent. "Notice there are no bright lines near *it.*"

"But suppose he finds out how to use it?" That was Hardie again.

"It would take months!" exclaimed "X." "You can't even make your little finger flexible in twenty-four hours."

There were more whispers, to which Thorson responded furiously, "Surely, you don't expect him to escape from *that* dungeon. Or have you been reading Aristotelian fiction, where the hero always wins?"

There was no question finally of who was going to have

his way. Men came and carried Gosseyn, chair, manacles, and all, down four flights of stairs into a solid-steel dungeon. The final stairs led down *into* the dungeon, and when the men had climbed back to the floor above, a motor lifted the whole staircase through a hole in the ceiling twenty feet above. A steel door clanged down over the hole, and heavy bars were slammed shut. There was silence.

V

Gosseyn sat still in the steel chair. His heart hammered, his temples throbbed, and every few moments he felt faint and ill with reaction. There seemed no end to the perspiration that poured from him.

"I'm afraid," he thought. "Horribly, wretchedly afraid."

Fear must derive from the very colloids of a substance. A flower closing its petals for the night was showing fear of the dark, but it had no nervous system to transmit the impulse and no thalamus to receive and translate the electric message into an emotion. A human being was a physico-chemical structure whose awareness of life was derived from an intricate nervous system. After death, the body disintegrated; the personality survived as a series of distorted impulse-memories in other people's nervous systems. As the years flew by, those memories would grow dimmer. At most, Gilbert Gosseyn would survive as a nerve impulse in other human beings for half a century; as an emulsion on a film negative for several score years; as an electronic pattern in a series of cathode-ray cells for perhaps two centuries. None of the potentialities diminished even fractionally the flow of perspiration from his body in that hot, almost airless room.

"I'm as good as dead," he thought in agony. "I'm going to die. I'm going to die." And even as he thought the words, he realized that his nerve was breaking.

A light flashed into brilliance on the ceiling; a metal slot was shoved open. A voice said, "Yes, tell Mr. Thorson he's doing fine."

Minutes passed, and then the stairway came rushing down. Its lower end clanged on the floor. Workmen began to edge down the stairs carrying a table. In quick succession the machine that had already been used on Gosseyn, and several others of different shape and purpose, were carted down and bolted to the table. The workmen retreated quickly up the stairs.

Two hard-faced men came down gingerly. They examined Gosseyn's hands and wrists. They went away, finally, and there was silence.

Then once more the door slid open metallically. Gosseyn shrank, expecting Thorson. Instead, Patricia Hardie came racing down the steps. As she unlocked the manacles, she said in a low, urgent tone, "Follow the hallway outside to the right for a hundred feet. Under the main staircase at that point you will see a door. Inside that door is a narrower stairway which leads up two flights to within twenty feet of my apartment. Perhaps you can hide there safely; I don't know. From this moment, you are on your own. Good luck."

Having freed him, she ran up the stairway ahead of him. Gosseyn's muscles were so cramped that he stumbled awkwardly on every step. But her directions had been sound. And by the time he reached the girl's bedroom, his circulation was back to normal.

A subtle aroma of perfume identified the bedroom suite. From the French windows, near the canopied bed, Gosseyn gazed at the atomic beacon of the Machine. It blazed so close that it almost seemed to him he could put forth his hand and grasp the light.

Gosseyn did not share Patricia Hardie's hope that he could hide safely in her bedroom. And besides, now before his escape was discovered, was the time to make the break. He started forward, and then drew back hastily as a half-dozen men with guns passed under the balcony in single file. When he peeked out a moment later, two of the men were crouching behind a line of shrubbery less than a hundred feet away.

Gosseyn retreated into the bedroom. It required no more than a minute to glance in at the four rooms that made up the girl's apartment. He chose the dressing room as his best vantage point. It had a window and a small balcony that opened on an alcove away from the main grounds. At worst, he could swing down and slip from shrub to shrub. He sat down heavily on the long bench before the huge, full-length mirror. Sitting there, he had time to wonder about Patricia Hardie's action.

She had taken a grave risk. The reason was obscure, but it seemed apparent that she regretted her participation in the plot against him.

The thought ended as a distant door clicked faintly. Gosseyn climbed to his feet. It might be the girl. It was. Her voice came softly a moment later at the dressing-room door.

"Are you in there, Mr. Gosseyn?"

Gosseyn unlocked the door without a word, and they stood facing each other across the threshold. It was the girl who spoke first.

"What are your plans?"

"To get to the Machine."

"Why?"

Gosseyn hesitated. Patricia Hardie had helped him, and so deserved his confidence. But he had better remember that she was a neurotic who had probably acted on impulse. She might not yet realize the full implications what she had done. He saw that she was smiling grimly.

"Don't be silly," she said, "and try to save the world. You can't do anything. This plot is bigger than Earth, bigger than the solar system. We're pawns in a game being played by men from the stars."

Gosseyn stared at her. "Are you crazy?" he said.

The moment he had spoken, he had a sense of blankness, a feeling of having heard words with too much meaning. He parted his lips to speak again, and then closed them. He recalled a word that Hardie had used earlier, "galactic." Then he had been too intent for it to penetrate. Now—His mind began to retreat from the vastness of what was here. It grew smaller and smaller, and fastened finally on one thing the girl had said.

"Men?" he echoed.

The girl nodded. "But don't ask me how they got there. I don't even know how men got to Earth. The monkey theory seems plausible only when you don't examine it too closely. But let's not go into that, please. I'm glad they're men, and not alien monsters. I assure you the Machine can do nothing."

"It might protect me."

She frowned over that, then said slowly, "It might at that." She studied him again with her bright eyes. "I don't understand where you fit into this. What did they find out about you?"

Gosseyn described succinctly what had been said, and added, "There must be something. The Machine also advised me to get my cortex photographed."

Patricia Hardie was silent. "By God," she said finally, "maybe they've got a right to be scared of you." She broke off. "Sh-sh, somebody's at the outer door."

Gosseyn had heard the musical chimes. He glanced back at the window. The girl said quickly, "No, don't go yet. Lock the door after me, and leave only if there's a search."

He heard her footsteps going away. When they came back, they were accompanied by heavier ones. A man's voice said, "I wish I'd seen the man. Why didn't you tell me what you were up to? Even Thorson is scared now."

The girl was calm. "How was I supposed to know he was different, Eldred? I talked to a person who had no memory of his past."

Eldred, Gosseyn thought. He'd have to remember the name. It sounded more like a Christian than a family name. The man was speaking again.

"If it were anyone but you, Pat, I'd believe that. But I always have the feeling that you're playing a private game of your own. For heaven's sake, don't be too clever."

The girl laughed. "My dear," she said, "if Thorson ever suspects that Eldred Crang, commander of the local galactic base, and John Prescott, the vice-commander, have both been converted to null-A, then you'll have a reason to talk about private games."

The man's voice sounded startled, hushed. "Pat, are you mad, even mentioning that? . . . But I've been intending to warn you. I no longer trust Prescott absolutely. He's been shifting and squirming ever since Thorson's arrival. Fortunately, I never let him find out about my feelings for null-A."

The girl said something Gosseyn did not catch. There was silence, followed by the unmistakable sound of a kiss, and then her voice. "Is Prescott going with you?"

Gosseyn was trembling. "This is silly," he thought angrily. "I was never married to her. I can't let a false belief disturb me emotionally." But the feeling was unmistakable. The kiss shocked him. The emotion might be false, but it would require more than one null-A therapy to break its hold on him.

The sound of the door chimes ended the thought. He heard the man and the girl go into the living room. Then the door opened and a man said, "Miss Patricia, we have orders to search this apartment for an escaped prisoner. . . . I beg your pardon, Mr. Crang. I didn't see you there."

"It's all right." It was the voice of the man who had kissed Patricia Hardie. "Complete your search and then depart."

"Yes, sir."

Gosseyn waited for no more. The balcony that led from the dressing-room window was tree-sheltered. He reached the ground without incident, and edged along the wall on his hands and knees. Not once, in those first few hundred yards, was he out of the shelter of a shrub or a tree.

He was a hundred feet from the almost deserted base of the Machine when a dozen cars careened from behind a line of trees, where they had been waiting, and guns opened fire at him. Gosseyn gave one wild shout at the Machine:

"Help me! Help!"

Aloof and unheeding, the Machine towered above him. If it was true, as legend said, that it was able to defend itself and its grounds, then there apparently was no reason for action. Not by a flicker of a tube did it show awareness of the outrage that was being done in its presence.

Gosseyn was crawling frantically along the grass when the first bullet actually struck him. It hit one shoulder and sent him spinning into the path of a burning energy beam. His clothes and flesh flared in an insanity of flame; and then he had rolled over and the bullets were focused again. They began to rip him apart as he burned with an incandescent fury.

The unbearable part was that he clung to consciousness. He could feel the unrelenting fire and the bullets searching through his writhing body. The blows and the flame tore at his vital organs, at his legs, his heart, and his lungs even after he had stopped moving. His last dim thought was the infinitely sad, hopeless realization that now he would never see Venus and its unfathomed mysteries.

Somewhere along there, death came.

VI

A curious, heavy sound impinged upon Gosseyn's attention. It seemed to come from above him. It grew louder rapidly and became a continuous noise, like the roar of many smoothly operating machines.

Gosseyn opened his eyes. He was lying in half darkness beside the trunk of a titanic tree. He could see two more trunks dimly in the near distance, but their size was so improbable that he closed his eyes and lay quiet, listening. He had no other immediate awareness. His brain was a composite of ears and what the ears were hearing. Nothing else. He was an inanimate object with the ability to detect sounds.

Further awareness crept in upon him. He could feel his body lying on the ground. No visual image was involved, but gradually the impression in his mind extended. Himself being held up by the soil of Venus, solidly, strongly supported by the impregnable planetary base that was Venus.

The slow flow of thoughts changed. Venus! But he wasn't on Venus. He was on Earth. Memory awakened in a remoter section of his mind. The trickle of impulse-patterns became a stream, then a wide, dark river rushing toward a great sea.

"I died," he told himself. "I was shot and burned to death."

He cringed with the remembrance of hideous pain. His body pressed hard against the ground. Slowly his mind opened out again. The fact that he was alive with the memory of having been killed became less a thing of remembered agony, more a puzzle, a paradox that had no apparent explanation in the null-A world.

The fear that the pain would resume dimmed with the passing of the uneventful minutes. His thought, in that

51

curious semiconscious world in which he had his momentary being, began to concentrate on different aspects of his situation.

He remembered Patricia Hardie and her father. He remembered "X" and the implacable Thorson, and that there was a plot against null-A.

The memory had an enormous, purely physical effect on him. He sat up. He opened his eyes and found himself in the same half darkness as before; it had not been a dream then.

He saw the monstrous trees again. This time he accepted them for what they were. It was they that must have given him his automatic knowledge that he was on Venus. Everybody knew about the trees on Venus.

He was definitely on Venus.

Gosseyn climbed to his feet. He felt his body. He seemed to be all right. There were no scars, no sense of having been wounded. His body was whole, well, undamaged. He was in perfect health.

He was wearing a pair of shorts, an open-necked shirt, and sandals. That astonished him, momentarily. He had been wearing trousers, with matching coat, the sober dress of the contestants in the games. He shrugged. It did not matter. Nothing else mattered, except that whoever had repaired his shattered body must have placed him here in this Gargantuan forest with a purpose. Gosseyn looked around him, as tense suddenly as he had been excited.

The trunks of the three trees that he could see were as thick as skyscraper buildings. He remembered that the famous Venusian trees were reputed to grow as high as three thousand feet. He looked up, but the foliage was impenetrable. Standing there, gazing upward, he grew aware that the sound which had awakened him had stopped.

He shook his head in puzzlement and he was turning away when there was a *whoosh* above him. A gush of water struck his head and poured over him.

The first gush was like a signal. All around him, water rushed down. He could hear the splashing in the shadows on every side, and twice more he was partially engulfed. Like a gigantic sprinkler system, the branches above were sending down torrents of water, and there was no longer any doubt what had happened.

It had rained. Enormous leaves had taken the load in their ample, up-curved, green bosoms. But now here, now there, the water was overweighing leaf after leaf and tumbling down into the depths, frequently into other leaves. But always the process must have continued until some small portion of the great bulk of water actually reached the ground. The rain must have been on a colossal scale. He was lucky to be in a forest the leaves of which could almost support a river.

Gosseyn peered around the bole of the tree near which he was standing. It was hard to see in the dim light, but it seemed to him finally that there was a greater brightness not far ahead. He walked toward it, and in two minutes he came to an open meadow. A valley spread before him. To his left he could see a wide, badly discolored river. To his right, perched on the rim of a hill, almost hidden by gigantic flowering shrubs, was a building.

A Venusian house! It nestled in its green environment. It seemed to be made of stone, and, what was more important, there was concealing shrubbery all the way from where he stood right up to its walls. He'd be able to approach it without being seen. This isolated house must be the reason that he had been left in this particular part of the forest.

The intervening brush fulfilled his expectations. Not once did he have to cross open ground. He reached a shrub that was ablaze with purple flowers, and from its shelter he surveyed the stone steps that led up through the terraced garden to the veranda of the house. There was lettering engraved on the bottom step. It was so sharply outlined that he could read it without difficulty.

JOHN AND AMELIA PRESCOTT

Gosseyn drew back. *Prescott.* He remembered the name. Patricia Hardie and Crang had used it in her apartment. "If Thorson ever suspected," the girl had said, "that Eldred Crang and John Prescott, commander and vice-commander, respectively, of the local galactic base, had become believers in null-A, then—" And then Crang had said, "I've been intending to tell you. I no longer trust Prescott absolutely. He's been shifting and squirming ever

53

since Thorson's arrival on Earth." That was the meaning of what they had said.

There it was. He knew who lived in the house. John Prescott, who had adopted the null-A philosophy intellectually, but had not yet made it an integral part of his nervous system. So he was wavering in the crisis.

It was something to know. It shaped his own attitude toward the man and woman up there. He began to edge upward through the mud of the terraced garden. He felt remorseless now. He himself had been handled without mercy and he would give none. He wanted information. About himself. About the things he needed to know about Venus. He would get it.

As he drew nearer the house, Gosseyn heard a woman's contralto voice. He paused behind a bushy shrub ten feet from the open veranda and peered around it cautiously.

A man with blond hair was sitting on the veranda steps making notations on a hand recorder. The woman stood in the doorway of the house. She was saying, "Well, I suppose I'll be able to manage alone. No patients are due until the day after tomorrow." She hesitated, then: "I don't wish to seem critical, John, but you're away so often that I hardly feel married any more. It's less than a month since you returned from Earth, yet now you want to be off again."

The man shrugged and, without looking up from his recorder, said, "I'm restless, Amelia. You know I have a high energy index. Until the mood passes, I've got to be on the move or build up silly frustrations."

Gosseyn waited. The conversation seemed to be over. The woman turned back into the house. The man sat several minutes longer on the steps, then stood up and yawned. He looked at ease, apparently unworried by what the woman had said. He was about five feet, ten inches tall. He seemed husky, but the appearance of strength wouldn't matter if he had never taken null-A muscular training. People who were not conditioned had difficulty understanding how strong human muscles could be when they were temporarily cut off from the fatigue center of the brain.

Gosseyn's decision was made. The woman had called the man John. And no patients were due for several days.

That was identification enough. This was John Prescott, galactic agent, pretending to be a doctor.

The woman's statement that nearly a month had passed since Prescott's return from Earth staggered Gosseyn. Patricia Hardie had said to Crang, "Is Prescott going with you?" She must have meant *to* Venus, for here he was. But the shortness of the time elapsed was confusing. Had it taken his body only a few weeks to recuperate from its desperate wounds? Or had Prescott made several trips to Earth?

Not, he realized, that it made any difference. What mattered right now was his attack. It must be made now, while Prescott stood unsuspecting here in this garden of his Venusian home.

Now!

The mud hindered Gosseyn's forward dash. Prescott had time to turn, time to see his assailant, time for his eyes to widen and for shock to register on his face. He even managed to launch the first blow. If Gosseyn had been a smaller man, less superbly muscled, it might have stopped him. But he wasn't. And Prescott did not get in a second blow. Gosseyn hit him three times on the jaw, and caught his limp body as he fell.

Swiftly he carried the unconscious man up the veranda steps, and paused beside the door. There had been scuffling sounds. The woman might come out to investigate. But there was no movement from inside the house. Prescott stirred against his arm and moaned slightly. Gosseyn silenced him with another blow and stepped through the open door.

He found himself in a very large living room. The room did not have a rear wall. It opened, instead, onto a broad terrace. There was a garden beyond, and then what seemed to be another valley almost lost in mist.

To his right was a staircase leading to the upper floor, and to his left another stairway descended to the basement. On either side were doors that opened into rooms. Gosseyn heard pans rattling in one of the rooms, and there was the tantalizing odor of food cooking.

He headed upstairs. At the top he found himself in a corridor with many doors leading from it. He pushed open the nearest one. It was a spacious bedroom, with a great curving window facing toward a grove of Cyclopean trees. Gosseyn lowered Prescott to the floor beside the bed, quickly tore a sheet into strips, and bound and gagged the unconscious man.

Tiptoeing cautiously, Gosseyn went down the stairs and into the living room. The continuing rattle of kitchen utensils relaxed his tensed nerves. Apparently the woman had heard nothing. Gosseyn crossed the living room, paused briefly while he decided what to do with her, and then he stepped boldly across the threshold into the kitchen.

The woman was serving food out of a series of electronic cookers. Gosseyn had a glimpse of a daintily set table in a little alcove, and then the woman saw him out of the corner of her eye. She turned her head in mild surprise. Her gaze jumped from his face to his muddy feet. "Oh, my gosh!" she said.

She set down the plate and faced him. Gosseyn hit her once and caught her as she sagged toward him. He felt without compunction. She might be innocent. She might know nothing of her husband's activities. But it was too dangerous to risk a struggle with her. If she was null-A and he gave her an opportunity, she would have enough physical stamina to break away from him and set off an alarm.

She began to writhe in his arms as he carried her up the stairs, but before she was fully awake, he had her bound and gagged and stretched out beside her husband. He left the two of them lying there and went out to explore the house. Before he could be sure that his victory was complete, he had to verify that no one else was around.

VII

To be acceptable as scientific knowledge, a truth must be a deduction from other truths.

Aristotle
The Nicomachean Ethics
circa 340 B.C.

It seemed to be a hospital. There were fifteen additional bedrooms, each complete with electronic and other standard hospital equipment. The laboratory and the surgery were in the basement. Gosseyn hurried from room to room. When he had finally convinced himself that no one else was around, he began a more careful search of the rooms.

He felt dissatisfied. Surely it wasn't going to be as easy as this. As he peered into clothes closets and riffled hastily through unlocked drawers, he decided that his best plan was to get the facts he wanted, then leave. The sooner he departed the less chance there was of someone else appearing on the scene.

All his rummaging failed to locate a weapon. The disappointment of that sharpened his sense of danger from an outside source. Finally, hastily, he went out onto the veranda in the front of the building and then the terrace in the rear. A quick look, he thought, to see if anyone was coming, and then questions.

There were so many questions.

It was the view from the terrace that delayed him. For he realized why he had been unable to see the valley that was there beyond the garden. From the edge of the terrace, he looked down, down, into the gray-blue haze of distance. The hill on which the hospital was built was not really a hill at all, but a lower peak of a mountain. He could see where the slopes leveled off. There were trees down there, too. They stretched for scores of miles and faded into the mists of remoteness. There were no mountains in that direction, so far as he could make out.

But that didn't matter. What seemed clear now was that this building could be approached only from the air. True, they could land a mile or more away, as he must have been landed, and then walk. But the air approach was an essential step in the process.

It was not particularly encouraging. One minute the sky could be empty except for the hazy atmosphere. The next a ship loaded with gang members could be settling down on the terrace itself.

Gosseyn drew a deep, slow, exhilarated breath. The air was still rain-fresh, and it braced him to acceptance of his danger. The very mildness of the day calmed his restless mind. He sighed and let the sweetness of the day tingle upon and through his body. It was impossible to tell what

57

time of day it was. The sun was not visible. The vast height of the sky was cut off by clouds that were almost hidden in the haze of an atmosphere that was more than a thousand miles thick. A hush lay over the day, a silence so intense that it was startling—but not frightening. There was a grandeur here, a peace unequaled by anything in his experience. He felt himself in a timeless world.

The mood passed more swiftly than it had come. For him, it was time that mattered. What he could learn in the shortest possible time might determine the fate of the solar system. He searched the sky in a quick last look. And then he went inside and up to his prisoners. His presence here was an unqualified mystery, but through them he had at least partial control of his situation.

The man and woman lay where he had left them. They were both conscious, and they looked at him with anxiety. He had no intention of harming them, but it wouldn't hurt to keep them jittery. He gazed down at them thoughtfully. In a sense, now that he was ready to concentrate on them, he was seeing them for the first time.

Amelia Prescott was dark-haired, slim, and good-looking in a very mature fashion. She wore a midriff blouse, shorts, and sandals. When Gosseyn removed her gag, her first words were, "Young man, I hope you realize that I've got a dinner on the stove."

"Dinner?" said Gosseyn involuntarily. "You mean it will be dark soon?"

She frowned at that, but did not answer directly. "Who are you?" she said instead. "What do you want?"

The questions reminded Gosseyn unpleasantly that he didn't know anything more about himself basically than she did. He knelt beside her husband. As he untied the gag, he studied Prescott's face. It was a stronger countenance, seen so closely, than he expected. Only positive beliefs could put that look on a man's face. The problem was, were his convictions rooted in null-A? Or did his strength derive from the certainties that a leader must cultivate?

He expected Prescott's comment on his predicament to furnish a clue to his character. He was disappointed. The man lay staring up at him, more thoughtfully now. But he said nothing at all.

Gosseyn faced the woman again. "If I should call Roboplane Service," he said, "what should I say to them to get a plane?"

She shrugged. "That you want a plane, of course." She looked at him, an odd expression on her face. "I'm beginning to understand," she said slowly. "You're on Venus illegally, and unfamiliar with everyday life here."

Gosseyn hesitated. "Something like that," he admitted finally. He returned to his problem. "I don't have to quote a registry number or anything like that?"

"No."

"I dial their number and say I want a plane? Do I tell them where to send it?"

"No. All public-roboplanes are connected with the dial system. That goes by pattern. The planes follow the electronic pattern and come to the videophone."

"There's absolutely nothing else to do?"

She shook her head. "No, nothing."

It seemed to Gosseyn that her replies were too frankly given. There was a way to settle that. A lie detector. He remembered having seen one in an adjoining room. He got it and set it up beside her. The lie detector said, "She's telling the truth."

To the woman, Gosseyn said, "Thanks!" He added, "How long will it take a plane to get here?"

"About an hour."

There was a video extension on the table near the window. Gosseyn sank into a chair beside it, looked up the number, and dialed it. The video plate on the earphone did not even flicker. Gosseyn stared at it, startled. He dialed again, hurriedly, and this time listened intently at the receiver. Dead silence.

He got up, and ran downstairs to the main instrument in the living room. Still no answer. He clicked open the door at the back and peered into the heart of the machine. It was normally warm. All the transparent tubes were glowing. The fault must be outside the building.

Slowly, Gosseyn climbed back to the second floor. There was a picture in his mind, a picture of himself cut off here on this mountain. Cut off physically and by the mystery of himself. It was a dark inward world at which he gazed. He felt depressed and tense. The idyl was over.

His belief that he was in control of the situation was meaningless in the face of what had happened to the videophone.

Somewhere out there the forces that had put him here were waiting. For what?

VIII

Gosseyn climbed slowly up the stairs. At the top he stopped to collect his thoughts. His plan for an easy departure had failed. He visualized the potentialities. He would get some information and then leave on foot as quickly as possible.

The decision braced him. He turned to go into the bedroom, but paused as the voice of Prescott came.

"What I don't understand is what happened to the video."

His wife sounded thoughtful. "It can only be one of two things. An interference screen has been set up between here and"—Gosseyn did not catch the name—"or else there's a fault in the machine itself."

"But isn't there supposed to be automatic warning long before anything is worn out, whereupon a repairman comes along and fixes it up?"

Gosseyn waited for the woman's reply to that. It was hard for him to believe they knew nothing about it.

"That's the way it's always been," said Amelia Prescott. "It seems very strange."

Gosseyn forced himself to wait for further comment. When none was made, he tiptoed hurriedly down the stairs, then came up again, noisily this time. The delay strained his patience, and, since he wasn't sure that the pretense would serve a useful purpose, he made up for lost time the moment he entered the room.

"Where," he asked, "do you keep your maps of Venus?"

Prescott did not reply, but his wife shrugged and said, "They're in a cupboard in the laboratory." She described the location of the cupboard.

Gosseyn remembered having looked into it. He hurried down into the basement and dug out three maps. Upstairs again, he spread them out on the floor and knelt beside them. He had seen maps of Venus before, but it was different being there. Besides, these were more detailed. Gosseyn looked up.

"Will you show me where you are on one of these things?"

The woman said, "We're on the one marked 'Three,' on that central mountain range. I once put a little mark showing our approximate location. It's probably still there."

Gosseyn found it about four hundred miles north of the city of New Chicago.

"Oh, there's ample fruit," she said in answer to his next query. "Purple berries an inch in diameter by the billion, a large yellow fruit, a bananalike juicy fruit, reddish in color. I could name a dozen others, but those are available the year round. They'll see you through any trip that you can possibly make."

Gosseyn studied the woman's face thoughtfully. Finally, he reached over and touched the lie detector. It said, "That's the way it is."

He turned back to Amelia Prescott. "You're convinced I'll be captured?" he asked. Briefly, he was intent. "Is that it?"

"Of course you'll be captured." She was calm. "We have no police system on Venus, and no ordinary crimes. But the cases requiring detective work that come up are always solved with extraordinary speed. You'll be interested in meeting a null-A detective, but you'll be shocked by the swiftness which which you are captured."

Gosseyn, whose main purpose was to contact Venusian authorities, was silent. He felt torn. His impulse now was to leave immediately. The sooner the concealing vastness of the mighty forest closed around him, the safer he would be. But Amelia Prescott's complete misunderstanding of the situation drew her character into sharper focus.

She was innocent. She was not a member of the gang. That seemed clear now.

Conversely, her husband's silence was abnormal. Thinking about it, Gosseyn felt himself change color. Until this moment he had taken it for granted that he was not recognized. Prescott had not been one of those present at the palace of the Machine on earth. But suppose the man had been shown photographs.

It changed things. He had decided earlier to give no explanations. But if Prescott knew him, then silence might make the man suspect that he himself was known.

On the other hand, it would be folly to identify himself as Gilbert Gosseyn if he didn't have to. He stood up. And then once more he hesitated. Abruptly he knew he couldn't depart without telling the woman. If anything happened to him, then she at least would know.

Through her the whole of Venus might be warned of the hideous danger that threatened. Telling her would be risky for her too, but Gosseyn had a plan for that. He would leave the decision about her husband up to her.

Gosseyn sat down on the edge of the bed. Now that he had made up his mind, he felt cool and unshakable. His nerves were steady as lead, that stable element. Ostensibly, then, he addressed himself to both the man and the woman. Actually, only the woman interested him. After a little more than a minute, Prescott rolled over and studied his face. Gosseyn pretended not to notice.

Twenty minutes later he let his voice lapse into silence. In the bright light that glared in through the wall window, he saw that Prescott's eyes were fixed on him.

"I suppose," the man said, "you realize your story has a basic flaw."

The man seemed to have forgoten his long silence, and Gosseyn accepted casually his entry into the conversation.

"My story," he said, "is true according to my memory. And any lie detector will bear out every word of it. That is, unless—" He paused, smiled bleakly.

"Yes?" Prescott urged. "Unless what?"

"Unless all the memory I now have is of the same category as my earlier belief that I had been married to Patricia Hardie, but that she had died, leaving me grief-stricken." He broke off sharply. "What is this flaw you have detected?"

The answer was thalamically prompt. "Your identification of your present self with the Gosseyn who was killed. Your complete memory of that death, the way the bullets and the energy struck you and hurt you. Think about that. And then think of the underlying credo of null-A, that no two objects of the universe can be identical."

Gosseyn was silent. Through the window, trees taller

than the tallest skyscrapers towered toward a blue haze of sky, and a swift river flowed through an evergreen world. Strange and tremendous setting for a conversation about the structural nature of things organic and inorganic, things molecular, atomic, electronic, neural, and physico-chemical, things as they were. He felt a deep wonder. Because *he* didn't seem to fit into that universe. A score of times since his awakening, he had thought of the very objection that Prescott was now making.

He was a man who claimed not merely similarity of structure but identification with a dead man. In effect, he was maintaining that because he had the memory and general physical appearance of Gilbert Gosseyn I, he was Gilbert Gosseyn I.

Any student of philosophy, even in the olden days, knew that two apparently identical chairs were different in ten thousand times ten thousand ways, none of them necessarily visible to the naked eye. In the human brain, the number of possible paths that a single nerve impulse could take was of the nature of ten to the twenty-seven-thousandth power. The intricate patterns set up by a lifetime of individual experience could not ever be duplicated. It explained beyond all argument why never in the history of Earth had one animal, one snowflake, one stone, one atom ever been exactly the same as another.

Unquestionably, the doctor had discovered a basic flaw in his story. But it was a flaw that, in itself, required weighty explanations. It was a flaw that could not be dismissed by a refusal to face it squarely.

Prescott was watching him narrowly. "I suppose," he said, "you realize that there is a lie detector in the room."

Gosseyn stared at him as a hypnotized bird might gaze at a snake. There was silence, except for a queer drumming sound at the back of Gosseyn's mind. He began to feel dizzy. His vision blurred. He sat cold and tense.

"It would be interesting," Prescott went on inexorably, "To find out if there really was another body."

"Yes," said Gosseyn at last, blankly. "Yes, it would be interesting."

Now that the words had been used, the picture presented to him this way, he didn't believe his story himself. He felt reluctant to put it to the test. Yet long before

Prescott had mentioned the detector, he had known there could be no evading its use. He went over to it. He put his hands on the metal contacts and waited while the sensitive energy-conducting lights played over his face.

"You've heard what we've been saying," he said. "What is your verdict?"

"It is impossible for me to prove or disprove your story. My judgments are based on memory flow. You have the memory of Gilbert Gosseyn I. That includes a memory of having been killed so realistically that I hesitate to say it couldn't have been death. There is still no clue as to your real identity."

For better or worse it was a moment for decision. Gosseyn bent down and untied the woman's feet though not her hands. He helped her stand up.

"My plan," he said, "is to take you with me for about a mile, then let you come back and release your husband."

He had another reason for taking her along. He intended to tell her what the situation was and what he had heard about her husband (though not that Patricia had said it), and so he would leave the problem of what to do with Prescott up to her.

He told her during the final quarter of a mile before untying her hands. When he had finished, she was silent for so long that he added finally, "Your husband may decide to prevent you from passing on the facts I've given you. On the other hand, his belief in null-A may be stronger than his loyalty to his government. You'll have to make up your mind about that from your own knowledge of him."

The woman sighed. But all she said was, "I understand."

"This hospital," said Gosseyn, "how does it work?" It was a point he wanted to clear up.

"It's all volunteer, of course," she said. "We're on Hospital Exchange. When somebody gets hurt or wants hospitalization, the robot exchange calls the nearest suitable unit. Then we accept or refuse the patient. Lately, I have been turning them down because—" She stopped. She looked at Gosseyn earnestly. "Thank you for everything. Thank you very much." She hesitated. "I intend to trust him," she said, "but I'll let you have a good start first."

"Good luck!" said Gosseyn.

He watched her as she started on the return journey. Woman the nurturer, he thought, woman the healer, the teacher, the understanding spirit, the lover. Woman! Not merely an imitation of man. In everything that he had seen her do and heard her say, she was a woman's woman in the fullest null-A sense—under terrific pressure now and accordingly low in energy, but even that could not conceal the warm-hearted human being underneath.

He came out of his reverie, and, turning on his heel, continued on his way toward the forest. The grass was soft beneath his feet, and there was still a sort of path, as if others less earnestly bent had walked this way, lightly, airily, and left an imprint of happy strolls through the dusk of warm and fragrant evenings.

The fragrance was lingeringly there, sweetly, deliciously there. The scent of growing greens was a thick perfume headily intermixed with the fresh feel of the afternoon rain. Gosseyn had the exhilarating conviction of an adventure begun in paradise. For a while there was the hissing swish of the river, near by now. But that faded as he entered the shadows under the titan trees.

Shadows. It was like coming into a cave from bright day. It was like a corridor that kept twisting, changing, curving, now opening up into great antechambers, now narrowing down to a pathless tangle of tall, spreading shrubbery, but always with a roof overhead to hide the sky. He realized it would be hard to sustain his sense of direction among the trees. But he had a compass, which should keep him on his general course. He could hope for no more than that.

He was still walking along in the apparently interminable forest when he noticed that the shadows around him were darkening. There was no question finally but that night was falling. He was just beginning to wonder if he would have to sleep under the trees when he emerged from behind a huge bole into a large, open meadow.

He found a grassy nook and he was settling himself when a plane winged silently over the edge of a near-by hill. It came down fifty feet away from him, and rolled to a stop. A light flashed on in its nose. It swung around with an easy gliding movement, and caught Gosseyn in a blaze of sunlike brilliance. Out of the brightness a voice came.

"Gilbert Gosseyn, I am not an enemy, but I cannot make any explanation until you are in the plane. To insure that you will get in without argument or delay, I call your attention to the half-dozen guns that are pointing at you. There is no escape."

Gosseyn saw the guns, snouted barrel ends that poked out of the fuselage, and followed his movements. So long as they were there, it didn't matter whether he believed or disbelieved that it was not an enemy. Without a word he went around to the side of the plane and climbed into the open door that was there. He had barely time to slip into the nearest seat. The door slammed. All the lights blinked out. The machine raced forward and became airborne. It climbed steeply into the night sky.

IX

Gosseyn watched the dark ground below become formless. Swiftly the world of giant trees and the mountain land were at one with the night. A uniform black enveloped the hurtling machine. Anywhere from three to five minutes ticked by, and then slowly the plane leveled off. The lights flashed on, and the voice of the roboplane said, "During the next ten minutes you may ask any questions you please. After that I must give you landing instructions."

It took a moment to adjust to that. *Any* questions. Gosseyn found his voice. The first question was easy enough.

"Who are you?"

"An agent of the Games Machine."

Gosseyn sighed with relief. Then: "Is the Machine speaking through you to me?"

"Only indirectly. The Machine can receive messages from Venus, but cannot itself broadcast on interplanetary wave lengths."

"You're on your own?"

"I have my instructions."

Gosseyn took a deep breath. "Who am I?"

He waited, every muscle tensed, and then sagged back in his seat as the roboplane answered, "I'm sorry, but you are wasting time. I have no information about your past, only about your present situation."

"Does the Machine know?" he persisted.

"If it does, it did not confide in me."

Gosseyn felt desperate. "But I've got to know something. What about my feeling that I was killed?"

"Your body," said the roboplane in its level voice, "was badly damaged and burned when you were killed. But I have no idea how you still happen to be alive." It broke off. "Mr. Gosseyn, I strongly urge you to ask your questions on the Venusian situation. Or perhaps you would like me to give you a rapid summary of the conditions that prevail here on the eve of the invasion of Venus."

"But damn it—" Gosseyn said furiously. He caught himself, conscious of the time he was wasting. "Yes," he said wearily. "Yes, that sounds like a good idea."

The voice began:

"To understand the political situation here, you must reach out with your mind to the furthest limits of your ideas of ultimate democracy. There is no president of Venus, no council, no ruling group. Everything is voluntary; every man lives to himself alone, and yet conjoins with others to see that the necessary work is done. But people can choose their own work. You might say, suppose everybody decided to enter the same profession. That doesn't happen. The population is composed of responsible citizens who make a careful study of the entire work-to-be-done situation before they choose their jobs.

"For instance, when a detective dies or retires or changes his occupation, he advertises his intention, or, in the case of death, his position is advertised. If he is still alive, people who would like to become detectives come to discuss their qualifications with him and with each other. Whether he is alive or dead, his successor is finally chosen as a result of a vote among the applicants."

In spite of himself, Gosseyn had a private thought at that point. It had nothing to do with the picture he was being given of life on Venus, the hopeful, fascinating picture of a super-civilization. It was personal to the roboplane, a concrete awareness that the machine was giving him as objective an account as he had ever heard.

The roboplane's voice kept on:

"You must now visualize a condition where more than half the applicants for all detective and judicial positions are agents of the gang. By a careful system of murders, they have managed to eliminate the more dangerous of the normal membership, and at present have virtual control of all key detective and judicial positions, as well as quantity control of both organizations. This was all done under the direction of Prescott, which is why he is suspect and—"

That was where Gosseyn interrupted. "Just a minute," he said. "One minute, please." He stood up, only vaguely aware that he did so. "Are you trying to tell me—"

"I'm telling you," said the roboplane, "that you cannot escape capture. You can see now why I had to put up interference against your use of the Prescott videophone. Since Thorson's arrival these false detectives have used their authority to tap the videophones of every dangerous person. This includes, so far as Thorson is concerned, his own subordinates. That is why you can expect no help from Crang. He has to show harshness, energy, and ruthlessness, or be removed from his command.

"But I must be brief. Your existence and the mystery of your mind potential has caused a great war machine to mark time, while its leaders frantically try to find out who is behind you. In all earnestness, therefore, I say, do not think you are being lightly asked to do what I now propose as your only logical action:

"You must let yourself fall into their hands. You must do this in the hope that they are so vitally interested in your special mental and physical make-up that they will allow you to live for several days at least, while they investigate your nervous system in detail, and with more care than last time.

"But now, here are your final instructions:

"In a few moments you will be landed beside the forest home of Eldred Crang. Go to him and tell him your story of the threat to null-A as if you do not know anything about him. Carry the pretense through to the last possible moment, but you must be the judge of your danger at any given moment."

The plane tilted downward. "Better hurry," it said, "and formulate your questions."

Gosseyn's mind made a leap, then recoiled before the

extent of his danger. He settled firmly back into his seat. This was not a moment for questions. The time had come to make a few things clear.

"I am not," he said grimly, "going to leave this plane and do anything so suicidal. Nowhere in all this is there a sign of a precaution taken for my safety. That's right, isn't it?"

"No precautions are being taken," admitted the roboplane. "You're on your own from the moment you land." It added quickly, "Don't underestimate the potentialities of a man who has been killed but is still alive."

"To hell with that," said Gosseyn harshly. "I'm not doing this, and that's final."

The roboplane was calm. "You have no choice. If you do not leave the plane of your own free will, I shall release a particularly unpleasant gas and drive you out. I must point out that the instructions I have given you are designed to save your life. You can ignore them at your peril. Remember, it is the opinion of the Games Machine that you will either surrender to the gang or be captured by them. Please think that over, Mr. Gosseyn, and if you have any further questions—"

Gosseyn said gloomily, "What is the purpose of letting me fall into their hands?"

"It is important," was the answer, "that they have a close look at a man whom they know to be dead."

There was a bump, then a bouncing motion that ended as the plane came to a full stop. "Out," said the voice. "Get out! I cannot remain here even a minute. Get out. *Quick!*"

Its tone impelled Gosseyn. He had no intention of being gassed. At the door he paused and half turned.

"Hurry," said the roboplane. "It is vital that no one suspect how you were brought here. Every second counts. Head straight away from the door."

Reluctant but obedient, Gosseyn stepped down to the ground. A moment later he was alone in the immense darkness of an alien planet.

X

The night was peaceful but dark. Gosseyn followed the directions of the roboplane, and he had proceeded scarcely a hundred yards when he saw a glimmer to his left. It was a vague reflection that grew brighter as he walked toward it. It became a glow that splashed the ground and lighted up neighboring trees. He saw its source finally. Massive shadows *in* a tree at the edge of the forest.

Gosseyn paused in the shadow of a towering shrub and gazed up the windows. Back inside the roboplane, except for his one outburst of resentment, he had made up his mind that he had to follow the advice of the Games Machine. He waited now, watching for figures to silhouette against the great windows. But the light did not change. There was not even a reflected movement from inside. Dissatisfied but determined, Gosseyn stepped into the light. He had already noticed a great stairway to his right, cut out of the solid trunk. He walked up the steps to a terrace that led to a closed ornate door. He knocked loudly.

At the end of a minte, it occurred to Gosseyn that despite the blazing lights there might be no one at home. Once more he knocked, and then he tried the handle. The door opened noiselessly, revealing a dimly lighted corridor, a corridor that had been cut out of the solid wood, highly polished, and then left in its natural state. It shone with a dull luster. It had an intricate design, resembling mahogany centerwood, but its coloring was like dark-walnut veneer.

Gosseyn took one flashing glance and had the picture of it. He stood briefly hesitant. It would be silly if a man who intended to surrender was shot as a lawless intruder. He knocked once more, on the inner side of the door this time. No answer. Light streamed through an open door at the end of the corridor. He walked toward it and found himself in a large, cozy living room which, like the corridor, had been carved out of the solid wood of the great tree.

It, too, was highly polished, but apparently a different finishing process had been used, for the wood was lighter.

The effect was of richness, a magnificence accentuated by the furniture and by a rug that was at least ninety feet long by sixty feet wide. It was from here, obviously, that the light that he had seen outside had come. Massive, gleaming windows curved spaciously along one entire wall the full length of the room. It had six doors leading from it and Gosseyn followed each one in turn. To a kitchen with pantries and cold rooms and breakfast nook leading off it. To five bedrooms, each with private bath, and with a doorway leading into a dark room that seemed to be an immense garden *inside* the tree.

By the time he emerged from the fifth bedroom, it was apparent that Eldred Crang was not at home. No doubt he would return in due course, but his absence now posed a psychological problem. Gilbert Gosseyn's decision was postponed. He remained uncommitted. Until Crang came home, a change of mind was possible. It left things unsettled. It would make for nerve wear, for unease, and for recurring doubts as to the advisability of staying here to be captured by an enemy when the people of Venus had yet to be warned of danger.

He came to doors that faced each other across a hallway at the rear of the apartment. He tried each in turn. As with all the other doors he had tested, they were unlocked. One opened into the kitchen; the other into darkness. The light from the hallway poured over his shoulder, and, after his eyes grew accustomed to the dimness, he saw that he was looking into a cavelike corridor. After a hundred and fifty feet, the light melted into shadow, but Gosseyn had the impression that the cave continued on into the depths of the tree bole.

He closed the door and went to one of the bedrooms, undressed, and took a bath in the adjoining bathroom. Refreshed and drowsy, he crawled under the smooth sheets. The silence around him was as complete as anything he had ever experienced. His thoughts turned inward to the mystery of Gilbert Gosseyn, who had once been killed and now lived again. Even the gods of old hadn't done any better than that. In the old, romantic days he could have turned out to be a prince, an important government agent, or the son of some rich merchant. But there weren't any special people in the null-A universe. True, there were rich men in great numbers, and presumably President Hardie's agents could be called government agents of a sort. But values had changed. People were people, normally born equal, requiring null-A training to integrate their intelligence. There were no kings, no archdukes, no supermen, traveling incognito. *Who was he that he was so important?*

He slept with that thought in his mind.

Gosseyn awakened with a start. The light of day shone through the open bedroom door from the corridor that led to the living room. He sat up, wondering if Crang had returned without noticing that he had a visitor. He climbed out of bed, washed noisily whistling loudly and tunelessly the while. He felt a little foolish. But it was important that he make his presence known, rather than startle someone who might shoot on sight.

He whistled furiously as he strode into the kitchen. Nor was he quiet about the way he peered into drawers and cupboards. He rattled pots and pans. He examined the well-stocked refrigerator, noisily pulling out containers. He brought a cup and saucer down from a shelf with a crash. He fried his bacon with a crackle and sputter of fat. And he ate gustily—bacon, toast, tea, and fresh Venusian fruit.

When he had finished breakfast, he was still alone. He left the kitchen and swiftly explored the apartment. The living room was bright with the daylight that blazed in through the great windows. None of the bedrooms, except his own, had been slept in. He opened the door that led into the great tree and along the corridor. It was as dark as it had been the night before. For a moment he hesitated, wondering if he should explore it. He decided against it finally, and returned to the living room. From the great windows there he saw that the house in the tree looked out on a green meadow. Part of that meadow formed a portion of a neatly arranged garden. The garden covered several acres and was terraced up toward the tree to some connection with the tree that he couldn't see from the living-room windows. It began, he discovered on investigation, inside the tree, about seventy feet inside. A mere chip that seventy feet was, out of such a mass of growing wood. But it made possible a fairyland garden. There were shrubs he hadn't seen in the wild state, aglow with flowers. Flowers as big as Earth trees, so colorful that they seemed to be giving off a light of their own. Venus must be an experimental paradise for botanists.

The beauty of the garden could not hold him long. Restlessly, he went back into the apartment. What to do while he waited for Crang? In the living room, he examined the books on the bookshelves. Several titles interested him: *The Aristotelian and Non-Aristotelian History of Venus, The Egotist on Non-Aristotelian Venus, The Machine and Its Builders,* and *Detectives in a World without Criminals.*

Reading proved too quiet an occupation at first. Gosseyn turned on the recorder and gradually settled down. He began to read in a more sustained fashion. He ate lunch with a book beside his plate. By evening he was even more relaxed. With considerable anticipation, he lifted a side of beef from a deep freezer and sliced off a thick steak. After dinner he picked up the volume on Venusian history. It told the story of the first men to walk on Venus late in the twentieth century. It described how the boiling hell of that atmosphere was tamed as early as the first quarter of the twenty-first century, of how ice meteorites from Jupiter were coasted into a close orbit around Venus, and of how as a result it rained for thousands of days and nights.

The ice meteorites ranged in size from ten to a hundred cubic miles; and when they had melted their huge volume of water down on the surface, and into the atmosphere, Venus had oceans and oxygen in its atmosphere. By 2081 A.D. the Institute of General Semantics, just then entering its governmental phase, realized the null-A potentialities of the bountiful planet. By this time, transported trees and other plants were growing madly. The Machine method of selecting colonists came a hundred or so years later, and the greatest selective emigration plan in the history of man began to gather momentum.

Population of Venus as of 2560 A.D.—119,000,038 males, 120,143,280 females, the book said. When he finally put it down, Gosseyn wondered if the surplus of females might explain why a null-A woman had married John Prescott.

He took *The Egotist on Non-Aristotelian Venus* to bed

with him. A note in the frontispiece explained that Dr. Lauren Kair, Ps.D., the author, would be practicing on Earth in the city of the Machine from 2559 A.D. to 2564 A.D. Gosseyn glanced through the chapter headings and finally turned to one captioned, "Physical Injuries and their Effects on the Ego." A paragraph caught his attention.

> The most difficult to isolate of all abnormal developments of the ego is the man or woman who has been in an accident that has resulted in injuries which do not immediately cause aftereffects.

Gosseyn stopped there. He hadn't known what he was looking for, but here at last was a concrete logicality about "X." "X," the frightfully injured, the abnormal ego that had developed unnoticed by psychiatrists whose duty it was to watch for dangerous individuals.

Gosseyn awakened the following morning in a silent house. He climbed out of bed, amazed that he was still undiscovered. He'd give Crang another day and night, he decided, then take positive action. There were several things he could do. A videophone call, for instance, to the nearest exchange. And the tunnel in the tree should be explored. ——

The second day passed without incident.

Morning of the third day. Gosseyn ate his breakfast hurriedly and headed for the videophone. He dialed "Long Distance" and waited, thinking how foolish he had been not to do it before. The thought ended as a robot eye took form on the video plate.

"What star are you calling?" the robot's voice asked matter of factly.

Gosseyn stared at it blankly and finally stammered, "I've changed my mind." He hung up and sank back into his chair. He should have realized, he thought shakily, that the galactic base on Venus would have a private exchange, and that they would have direct communication with any planet anywhere. What *star*? For these people long distance meant long!

He studied the dial again and put his finger in the slot marked "Local." Once more a robot eye looked at him.

Its voice answered his request unemotionally. "Sorry, I can put no outside calls through from that number except from Mr. Crang himself."

Click!

Gosseyn climbed to his feet. The silence of the apartment flowed around him like a waveless sea. It was so quiet that his breathing was loud and he could hear the uneven beating of his heart. The voice of the robot operator again echoed in his brain. *"What star?"* And to think that he had wasted time. So much to do. The tunnel first.

He stood, a few minutes later, peering along the dim corridor that led into the depths of a tree that was an eighth of a mile thick and half a mile tall. It was very dark, but there was an atomic flashlight in the kitchen storeroom. Gosseyn secured the flash. He left the tunnel door open behind him. He began to walk along the low-roofed corridor into the interior of the tree.

XI

There was a drabness about his surroundings that dulled thought. The tunnel became winding and tilted more sharply downward. The curving walls gleamed vaguely in the light of the flashlight. Twice, during the first ten minutes, the tunnel divided in two. During the next hour, seven tunnels joined the one he was in, and three times more the corridor split ahead of him. It could have been confusing, but Gosseyn sketched a map in his notebook, ticking off each side tunnel.

"I must," he thought finally, "be walking several hundred feet below the ground, following the intertwining roots. I'm actually under the forest."

He had not thought before of the extent of the roots supporting the mighty trees. But here in this continuous maze was evidence that the roots were at once large in size and pressing in, one upon the other, so tightly that it was impossible to decide from inside the tunnel where the connections were, where one root left off and another began. He examined the next side tunnel for markings. There was nothing visible. The wood, lemon-colored here in the nether roots, curved solidly up to a solid ceiling. As far as his fingers could reach, he fumbled over the metallically hard surface. And there were no switches, no hidden panels, no directions of any kind.

He was disturbed now. These tunnels apparently were endless. He'd need food if he was really going to investigate them, as he must. Too bad he had to retrace two hours of walking. But better two hours than five. The time to turn back was before he began to feel hungry or thirsty.

He reached Eldred Crang's apartment without incident. He made a pile of meat sandwiches and was sitting down to a lunch of eggs and bacon when the four men came in. They entered through three different doors. The first three men held guns, and they came in as if they had been catapulted by the same tight-wound spring. The fourth man was a wiry chap with hazel eyes. He had no gun and he entered in a more leisurely fashion. It was he who said, "All right, Gosseyn, put up your hands."

Gosseyn, sitting rigidly at the table, head twisted up and around, presumed that Eldred Crang, galactic agent, Venusian detective, and secret supporter of null-A, had come home at last.

His first reaction was relief. Until responsible people with null-A training knew the danger that civilization faced, Gilbert Gosseyn must hold his life in trust. He tried to think of the coming of Crang as precipitating movement in that direction. He climbed to his feet, hands raised above his head, and watched the men curiously, trying to saturate his senses with the reality of their presence. He felt undecided as to how best he might tell them the story the Machine had urged upon him.

As he studied the men, one of them walked forward and broke open the package of sandwiches. They spilled out in a brown and white array, two falling on the floor with a vague sound, like pieces of dry dough. The man didn't speak immediately. But he smiled as he stared down at the sandwiches. He was a thickset, nicely groomed individual in his early thirties. He moved over to Gosseyn.

"Going to leave us, were you?"

His voice had a faint foreign tone to it. He smiled again. He hit Gosseyn stingingly across the face with the flat of his hand. He repeated in a dead-level tone, "Leaving, were you?"

He drew his hand back again. From Gosseyn's left, Crang said, "That's enough, Blayney."

The man lowered his arm obediently. But his face worked, and his voice was blurred by emotion as he said, "Mr. Crang, suppose he'd gone? Suppose he hadn't rung up exchange? Who'd have thought of searching for him here? Why, if he had escaped, the big boss would have—"

"Silence!"

Blayney subsided sullenly. Gosseyn turned to the wiry-bodied leader.

"If I were you, Crang, I wouldn't trust Blayney after he gets to be forty."

"Eh?" That was Blayney, an astounded look on his face. Crang's yellow eyes questioned Gosseyn.

"There are psychiatrical explanations for Blayney hitting me as he did," Gosseyn explained. "His nervous system is beginning to react as strongly to things that might have happened as it would if they had actually occurred. It's a purely functional disorder, but its outward form is distressing to the individual. A gradual loss of courage. Sadistic outbursts to cover up the developing cowardice. By the time he's forty he'll be having nightmares about the damage he might have suffered in some of the danger spots he was in as a youth." He shrugged. "Another case of a person lacking null-A integration."

Blayney had gray eyes. They glared at Gosseyn, then twisted over to Crang. He said in a hushed voice, "May I hit him again, Mr. Crang?"

"No. What do you care what he thinks?"

Blayney looked dissatisfied, and Gosseyn said nothing more to aggravate the situation. It was time to tell his story.

Surprisingly, they listened intently. When Gosseyn had finished, Crang took a cigarette out of a case and lighted it. He caught Gosseyn's gaze on him, but he said nothing immediately. There was a slightly baffled expression on his face, and after a minute he was still puffing wordlessly at the cigarette. Gosseyn had time to study the man.

Eldred Crang was a lean man but not tall. There was a dark quality about his appearance that suggested Middle

Eastern or Mediterranean origin. He had possibly been born on a planet with a hotter sun than Sol. His manner was restless, and that, with his yellow-green eyes, gave a sort of fire to his personality.

So this was the man whom Patricia Hardie loved. Gosseyn wondered if he ought to feel any emotional dislike. He didn't. Instead, he found himself remembering what the roboplane had said, that Crang could not be expected to be helpful. The man was surrounded by gang adherents and by his own people. With Thorson in over-all command, Crang would have to watch himself very carefully.

The man's silence ended abruptly. He laughed. "Just for a minute," he said, "I had a mind to let you get away with that story. But the truth is we don't have to play games. We've decided to have a general conference about you with you present. We leave for Earth within the hour."

"Earth!" said Gosseyn.

His lips twisted wryly. Since his arrival on Venus, he had succeeded in letting one person know about the threat to the solar system. And at most that person, Amelia Prescott, had passed his story on to Detective Registry, not knowing that organization was now little more than an appendage of the gang. One human being out of two hundred million. Crang was speaking again.

"All right, Blayney," he commanded, "bring in the Prescotts."

Gosseyn started, then controlled himself. He watched curiously as John and Amelia Prescott were brought in, handcuffed and gagged. The man stared stolidly across the room at his erstwhile captor, but his wife looked shocked as she saw Gosseyn. For a moment she actually fought the gag. Her eyes twisted with the effort. She subsided gloomily and shook her head helplessly at Gosseyn.

He gazed at her with pitying eyes. Here was the result of her decision to trust that her husband was more null-A than gang. Prescott had failed her. If she had been a member of the group they wouldn't have gagged her. She would have been able to carry through the appearance of being a prisoner without needing to be restrained from speaking.

It must be annoying to her husband, that he too had to

78

be gagged. And whatever the purpose of the farce, Gilbert Gosseyn had better play along with it. He knew who Prescott was, and they didn't know that he knew. It was one of his few advantages in a game where the cards were otherwise heavily stacked against him.

XII

Through the vast dark rushed a spaceship with one woman and four hundred and two men aboard. Crang gave Gosseyn the figures on the second day out.

"I have orders," he said, "to take no chances with you."

Gosseyn made no comment. He was puzzled about Crang. The man obviously intended to cling to his position in the gang, regardless of his belief in the philosophy of null-A. It would necessitate unpleasant compromises, and even a remorseless attitude where individual lives were at stake. But if he intended in the long run to use his power for null-A, then all the intermediate concessions to the gang would be compensated for.

Crang passed on along the promenade. Gosseyn stood for a long time peering through one of the mammoth forward portholes out into the interplanetary night. There was a supernally bright star in the darkness ahead. Tomorrow it would take on the contours of earth. And tomorrow evening he would be inside the official residence of President Hardie, after a voyage in space of three days and two nights.

The landing was a disappointment to Gosseyn. Mists and clouds ringed the continents, and all the way down through the atmosphere of Earth those clouds hid the land below. And then—final disappointment—a blanket of fog lay over the city of the Machine covering all that the clouds had missed. He had a tantalizing glimpse of the atomic light that was the Games Machine's own dazzling beacon. And then the spaceship sank down into the cavernous interior of a gigantic building.

Gosseyn was whisked off into the gathering fog-ridden twilight. The street lamps came on, and were mist-blurred blobs of light. The courtyard of the presidential palace was deserted, but it came alive with the sounds of men who poured out of the escort cars and surrounded him. He was herded into a long, brightly lighted corridor and up a flight of stairs into a luxurious hallway. Crang led the way to a door at the far end.

"Here we are," he said. "This will be your apartment while you remain a guest of the president. The rest of you remain outside, please."

He opened a door into a living room that was at least twenty feet long and forty wide. There were three other doors leading into it. Crang indicated them.

"Bedroom, bathroom, and back entrance. There's another door inside the bedroom joining it to the bathroom." He hesitated. "You will be neither locked in nor guarded, but I wouldn't try to get away if I were you. You couldn't possibly get out of the palace, I assure you."

He grinned. It was an engaging grimace, and quite friendly.

"You'll find suitable dinner clothing in the bedroom. Do you think you could be ready in about an hour? I want to show you something before dinner."

"I'll be ready," said Gosseyn.

He undressed, thinking of the opportunities for escape. He didn't accept Crang's statement that it would be impossible to get away, if they really had no guards around. He wondered if they were trying to tempt him.

There were several suits of clothing in the clothes closet of the bedroom, and he had selected one that was made up of a dark but shiny material when he heard a door open. He slipped into his dressing gown and went out into the living room. Patricia Hardie was in the act of closing the door which Crang had called the back entrance. She whirled with a lithe movement and came toward him.

"You damned fool!" she said without preliminary. "Why did you leave so fast when those guards came into my apartment? Didn't you hear me tell them I didn't allow my rooms to be searched on Thorson's orders?" She made a movement with her hand, a silencing movement. "Never mind. It's past. You did leave, got yourself killed, and now here you are again. That *was* you that was killed, wasn't it? It wasn't only a chance resemblance?"

Gosseyn parted his lips. She cut him off.

"I can only stay a minute. Believe me, I'm suspect number one in your escape last month, and if I'm caught up here——" She shuddered convincingly. "Gosseyn, who are you? You must know by now."

He studied her, infected by her excitement. She brought an aliveness into the room that had been missing. Her very breathlessness was intriguing.

"Tell me," she said imperiously. "Quick!"

It was easy enough to tell her what he knew. He had awakened on Venus without memory of how he had gotten there. He had nothing to hide of subsequent events except his knowledge that Prescott was of the gang. Even that Patricia knew, for she had loudly made the identification within his hearing. It was the one fact, however, that he could not mention aloud. If dictaphones were listening to this conversation, that was a secret which they must share in silence.

But everything else he told her, succinctly. Before he finished, she flung herself into a chair and bit her lips in obvious vexation.

"This second body of yours," she said finally, "actually knows nothing more than the first. You're really just a pawn."

Gosseyn stood looking down at her. He couldn't decide whether to be annoyed or amused. He was not prepared to go into the problem of two Gosseyn bodies with her, though he had had a few thoughts on the subject. The reference to his being a pawn stung, because it was true.

"Look," he said shortly, "where do you fit into all this?"

The girl's eyes softened. "I'm sorry," she said. "I didn't mean to hurt your feelings. The truth is that your very lack of knowledge has startled all groups. Thorson, the personal representative of Enro, has postponed the invasion of Venus. There! I thought that would interest you. But wait! Don't interrupt. I'm giving you information which I intended to give you a month ago. You'll want to know about 'X.' So do the rest of us. The man has a will of iron, but no one knows what his purpose is. He seems to be primarily interested in his own aggrandizement, and he has expressed the hope that some use can be made of you. The Galactic League people are bewildered. They

81

can't decide whether the cosmic chess player who has moved you into this game is an ally or not. Everybody is groping in the dark, wondering what to do next."

She paused. Her eyes were bright and excited. "My friend," she said, "there must be an opportunity for you in all this confusion. Take it." She was suddenly earnest. "Take it if it is offered and hasn't got impossible conditions attached to it. Stay alive."

She was on her feet. She touched his arm in a gesture of friendliness, and half ran to the door. In the open doorway she paused.

"Good luck!" she said, and shut the door behind her.

Gosseyn had his shower, thinking, "How does she know what all these people do and believe? Who is *she?*" When he came out of the bathroom, he saw that he had another visitor. President Hardie sat in one of the chairs.

The man's noble face lighted as he saw Gosseyn. Sitting there, he looked strong and calm and determined, an idealized version of a great man. He fixed his steady gaze on Gosseyn's face.

"I had this suite prepared for you," he said, "because I wanted to talk to you without fear of being overheard. But there is no time to waste."

"Isn't there?" said Gosseyn.

He spoke with deliberate hostility. This man had permitted a gang to make him president by a method which subverted the games of the Machine. The crime was collossal, unforgivable, and personal.

The fine face of the older man broke into a faint smile. "Come now," said Hardie. "Let us not be juvenile. You want information. So do I. You ask three questions, then I'll ask three." A pause. Then sharply, "You must have questions, man."

Gosseyn's hostility collapsed. He had more questions than he could ask in an evening. There was no time to waste.

"Who are you?" he asked pointedly.

Hardie shook his head regretfully. "I'm sorry," he said. "I am either what I appear to be or I am not. If the latter, then for me to tell you would put me at your mercy. A lie detector could get the information out of you."

He finished curtly, "Don't take up time with questions

that might destroy me. Now hurry."

"Do you know anything about me other than what has already been told?"

"Yes," said President Hardie.

He must have seen the look that came into Gosseyn's face, for he added quickly, "Not much, frankly. But a few days before you appeared on the scene, I received a letter in my personal mail. It was mailed here in the city of the Machine, and it indicated that the author knew all the details of what we had considered the best-kept secret in the solar system—the author knew about the attack being planned against Venus. After giving the whole story in brief, the letter went on to state that you would be staying at the Tropical Park Hotel and that you would prevent the attack on Venus.

"There was certain information in the letter which I did not care to have the others see, so I burned it and had you brought to the palace through the complicated procedure of which you already know. There you are. Now, question three."

"Two!" corrected Gosseyn.

"Three. If I ask a question you refuse to answer, it will count against me. Fair?"

His protest had been automatic. His mind was on what Hardie had said. He did not doubt the story. The reality could have been something like that. What was behind it, of course, was another matter.

Gosseyn studied the older man, impressed for the first time. The President was only one of a diverse group of highly capable plotters, each with his own purposes. But it was his personal achievement that he had persuaded men as egotistical as himself to give him the highest nominal position. The man's character, which he had scarcely thought about before, suddenly proved more intricate.

"Gosseyn, your next question!"

He had forgotten that speed was important. And besides the conviction was already on him that he was not going to learn much. These people didn't know enough. He said, "What's going to happen to me?"

"You will be made an offer, just what I don't know yet. Thorson and 'X' are talking it over. Whatever it is, I think you would be advised to accept it for the time being.

Mind you, you're in a strong position. Theoretically, if you can have two bodies, then why not a third?" He frowned. "Still, that's a speculation."

Gosseyn had stopped believing that he had ever had two bodies. He parted his lips to say so scathingly, and then closed them again. His eyes narrowed. These people must have some purpose in trying to put over an idea like that. It all seemed obscure and meaningless, but he mustn't forget that he had never actually been out of the control of the gang. Even the roboplane which claimed to be an agent of the Machine could have been carefully coached to give that impression. He'd better await developments.

He looked at Hardie and said aloud simply, "Yes, it's a speculation."

"My first question," said Hardie, "has to do with the man or group who is behind you. Has anyone claiming to be the representative of such an individual contacted you?"

"Definitely not. Unless the Machine is responsible, then I'm absolutely in the dark."

Hardie said, "Your belief about that does not make it so." He smiled. "Now you've got me making null-A statements. I've noticed the others do it, too. Even as we plot to destroy the null-A philosophy, we adopt its logic. 'The map is not the territory.' Your belief that you know nothing is an abstraction from reality, not the reality itself."

He paused. He sat quiet for a moment smiling with amusement, then said, "Question two: Have you any feeling in yourself of being different from other human beings?" He shrugged. "I admit that's an unsemantic question, because you can only know by observation what other people are like and your observations my be different from my own. We live in private worlds. Still, I can't describe it better than that. Well?"

This time Gosseyn found the question not only acceptable but profoundly interesting. Here were his own thoughts being put into words.

"I feel no difference in myself. I assume you mean the discovery made about my brain by Thorson." He broke off, tense. "What is there about my brain?"

He leaned forward. His body felt cold and hot by turns. He sighed as Hardie said, "Wait your turn. I still have my third question. What I want to know is, how did you find Crang's hideout?"

"I was taken there by a roboplane, which forced me to go along."

"Whose roboplane?" said Hardie.

"It's my question, thank you," said Gosseyn. "I think maybe we'd better each ask a question at a time. What's in my brain?"

"Additional brain matter. I know nothing of its nature. Thorson has come to discount its possibilities."

Gosseyn nodded. He was inclined to agree with Thorson. From the beginning he had felt not the slightest "difference."

"Whose roboplane?" Hardie repeated.

"It implied that it represented the Machine."

"Implied?"

"My question," said Gosseyn.

Hardie scowled. "You're not anwering your questions completely. Didn't it give you any evidence?"

"It knew several things that the Machine knows, but it urged me to surrender. I regard that as suspicious."

Hardie was thoughtful. "I see your point. And I can't clear that up for you. Crang dominates Thorson these days, and I am in the dark on many things. I'm afraid"—he smiled ruefully—"I'm being relegated."

So that was why he was here, offering facts on an equal exchange basis. Gosseyn had a sudden vivid picture of these Earthmen beginning to realize that they had been pawns. Before he could speak, Hardie said harshly, "I regret nothing, if that's what you're thinking. The Machine denied me the right to further advancement, and I refused to accept any such limitation."

"Why did it deny you?"

"Because it saw in me a potential dictator, so it said. The damned thing was set to weed out people like me at a time when there was still legitimate fear of such an eventuality."

"So you proceeded to prove that it was right?"

"The opportunity came, and I took it. I'd do the same

thing again, under the same circumstances. There'll be a place for me in the galactic hierarchy. Thorson is just playing safe now, in this crisis."

The grim expression faded from his face. He smiled. "We're getting away from our subject and—"

There was an interruption. The door opened, and a man in uniform entered hastily and shut the door behind him.

"Sir," he said to Hardie, "Mr. Thorson is climbing the stairs. I just received the signal."

President Hardie stood up. He looked annoyed but calm. "Well, that ends that. But I think I've learned what I wanted to know. I've been trying to make up my mind about you. It's clear to me that you are not the final Gosseyn. Good-by, and remember what I said. For the present, make compromises. Stay alive."

He and the guard went out the door through which Patricia had disappeared fifteen minutes earlier. They were gone only a few seconds when there was a knock on the main corridor door. Then the door was pushed open, and Thorson came in.

XIII

The big man paused on the threshold, and he was as Gosseyn remembered him, heavy-faced, hawk-nosed and strong. From the beginning, Thorson's position had been unmistakable—the man everyone feared, agent of Enro. Now his somber eyes surveyed Gosseyn.

"Not dressed yet!" he said sharply.

His gaze darted over the room. His eyes were suspicious. And in that mood, Gosseyn saw the man suddenly in another light. From the stars he had come into a strange sun system. Here on Earth, surrounded by people he did not know, acting under a directive from a remote authority, he was trying to carry out his instructions. The strain was transparently terrific. At no time could he be certain of the loyalty of the people with whom he had to co-operate.

He sniffed the air now. "Interesting perfume you use," he commented.

"I hadn't noticed," said Gosseyn. His attention having

86

been called to it, he detected a faint scent. He wondered if it belonged to Patricia. She'd have to watch out for little things like that. He stared at the big man stonily. "What do you want?"

Thorson made no effort to come further into the room, nor did he shut the door. He studied Gosseyn thoughtfully.

"I just wanted to have a look at you," he said. "Just look at you." He shrugged finally. "Well, that's that."

He turned and went out. The door closed behind him. Gosseyn blinked. He had been tensing for a verbal clash and he felt let down. He continued his dressing, puzzled by the man's action. He forgot it as he saw by the bedroom clock that it was almost time for Crang to come back. A moment later he heard the outer door open.

"Be right with you," he called.

There was no answer and no sound. A shadow darkened the door. Gosseyn looked up with a start. John Prescott came into the bedroom.

"I've only got a minute," he said.

In spite of his surprise, Gosseyn sighed. The uniform haste of his visitors was becoming tiresome. But he said nothing, simply climbed to his feet and looked at the man questioningly.

"You'll be wondering about me," said Prescott.

Gosseyn nodded, but his mind was almost blank. He listened silently to the rapid explanation that followed. It was all there. Galactic agent. Secret supporter of null-A. "Naturally," said Prescott, "I wasn't going to tell you that unless I had to. I recognized you from photographs when you were attacking me that afternoon, and, frankly, I reported your presence on Venus, taking it for granted that you would be able to get away. I was startled when you turned up at Crang's tree house."

He paused for breath and Gosseyn had time to feel disappointment. His one advantage over the group, that he knew about Prescott, was gone. It seemed silly in retrospect that he had ever counted on it to help him, but he had. The only question that remained was, what was the purpose of a confession at this hour?

"It's Amelia," Prescott said anxiously. "She's innocent in all this. I submitted to that farce of being a fellow captive with her, thinking they would merely hold her until the attack on Venus was made. But Crang told me a few minutes ago that 'X' and Thorson have something in mind for her in connection with you."

He stopped. With fingers that trembled ever so slightly, he drew a little metal box from his pocket, opened it, and, walking over, held the box out to Gosseyn. Gosseyn stared down curiously at the twelve white pills that were in it.

"Take one," said Prescott.

Gosseyn had a suspicion of what was coming, but he reached dutifully into the box and lifted out one of the pills.

"Swallow it!"

Gosseyn shook his head. He was annoyed. "I don't swallow strange pills."

"It's for your own protection. I swear it. An antidote."

"I haven't taken any poison," said Gosseyn patiently.

Prescott closed the box in his hand with a snap. He slipped it into one pocket, backed away, and simultaneously drew a blaster with his other hand. "Gosseyn," he said quietly, "I'm a desperate man. You swallow that pill or I'll burn you."

The danger was unreal. Gosseyn looked down at the pill, then at Prescott. He said mildly, "I noticed a lie detector in the next room. That would settle this very quickly."

It did. Prescott said to the lie detector, "This pill is an antidote, a protection for Gosseyn in case I take certain action. Will you verify that one point?"

The answer was prompt. "That's right," said the instrument.

Gosseyn swallowed the pill, stood for a moment waiting for effects. When none occurred, he said, "I hope everything will be all right with your wife."

"Thanks," was all Prescott said. He departed hastily by the door that led to the main corridor. Gosseyn finished dressing and then sat down to wait for Crang. He was more disturbed than he cared to admit. The people who had come to see him had been intent each in his own purpose. But one thing they had in common—an earnest belief that a crisis was imminent.

Venus was to be attacked—by whom was not clear. A

great galactic military power? It was strangely easy to picture, because this was the way it would be. This was the way that a race bound to its own sun and planets would be subjugated. Mysterious agents, meaningless actions, infiltration, and finally an irresistible attack from nowhere. The various references to a league of galactic powers opposed to the assault seemed vague and insubstantial beside the fact of the presence of Thorson and the steps that had already been taken. Murder. Betrayal. Seizure of power on Earth.

"And I'm supposed to stop it?" said Gosseyn aloud.

He laughed curtly, feeling ridiculous. Fortunately, the problem of himself was slowly untangling. For him, one of the most dangerous periods had been his partial acceptance of the propaganda that he had come to life again in a second Gosseyn body. At least his logic was slowly disposing of that. He could face the evening with his mind closer to sanity.

A knock on the door drew him out of his uneasy reverie. To his relief it was Crang.

"Ready?" the man asked.

Gosseyn nodded.

"Then come along."

They went down several flights of stairs and along a narrow corridor to a locked door. Crang unlocked it and pushed it open. Through it, Gosseyn had a glimpse of a marble floor and of machines.

"You're to go in alone and look at the body."

"Body?" said Gosseyn curiously. Then he got it. *Body!*

He forgot Crang. He went in. The larger view of the room disclosed more machines, some tables, wall cabinets lined with bottles and beakers, and in one corner a longish shape lying on a table, covered by a white sheet. Gosseyn stared at the sheeted figure and a considerable portion of his remaining calm began to slip from him. For many days he had heard talk of this other body of his, and, while the verbal picture he had conjured so often had affected him, there was a difference.

It was the difference between a thought and an event, between words and reality, between death and life. So mighty was that difference that his organs experienced a profound metabolic change, and his nerves, unable to integrate the new reactions, began to register wildly.

Bodily sanity came back with a rush. He grew aware of the floor pressing against his feet, and of the air of the room, cool and dry as ashes, in his lungs and in his mouth. His vision blurred. Slowly, conscious again of his humanness but still not normal, he let his mind float out toward that still, dead form. And though he had no consciousness of any movement, he walked to the body, reached forward, and, with the tips of his fingers, lifted the sheet and dragged it off the body onto the floor.

XIV

Gosseyn had expected to see a hopelessly charred body. In some respects, the corpse that sprawled rigidly on its back on the marble table was horribly damaged, but it was the body, not the face that had suffered. They must have had orders, the men who had fired at him, not to injure the brain. The body had been ripped almost in two by machine-gun bullets. The chest and abdomen were little more than tattered flesh and bone, and every ragged strip, every square inch of flesh above the knees was burned so terribly that there was no human resemblance. The face was intact.

It was a serene countenance, untouched by the fear and unendurable anguish that had racked it in those moments before death came. There was even a touch of color in the cheeks, and, if it hadn't been for the blasted body, it might have been himself sleeping there, so lifelike was the face. Undoubtedly precautions had been taken to prevent the brain from deteriorating. After a moment, he noticed that the top of the head was not actually attached to the skull. It was there, but it had been neatly sawed off and temporarily replaced. Whether the brain was still inside, Gosseyn did not attempt to find out.

A sound behind him made him straighten slowly. He did not turn immediately, but his mind began to lift clear of the dead body and to recognize in greater detail his general situation. It took several seconds before he identified the sound with a memory of other similar sounds. Rubber wheels on marble. "X." He looked around with the cold determination of a man who has braced himself for anything.

He stared icily at the plastic monstrosity. Then he turned his attention to the people who had followed "X" into the laboratory. Bleakly he looked straight into the eyes of the handsome Hardie. His gaze passed on to meet the cynical smile of the giant, Thorson, and finally to where Patricia Hardie, cool and interested, half-hidden behind the two men, watched him with her bright eyes.

"Well!" It was "X," bass-voiced and without humor. "I have an idea, Gosseyn, that you haven't the faintest plan for stopping us from laying you out cold beside your other body."

It was not a brilliant analysis, but it had one very important quality about it from the viewpoint of a man who had no belief at all that the essence of his personality would recur in a third body if this second one was destroyed. The important quality was that, word for word, it was the truth. "X" was waving his plastic arm with a gesture that suggested impatience. His next words confirmed it.

"Enough of this tomfoolery. Bring in the Prescott woman and hold Gosseyn."

Four men held Gosseyn as the woman was brought in by three huge guards. They looked as if they had been in a fight. Amelia Prescott's hair was down and her face flushed. Her hands were tied behind her back and she was breathing heavily. There must have been a transparent plastic gag inside her mouth, because her lips worked frantically in futile effort when she saw Gosseyn. She subsided finally, shrugging. She smiled at him a little sadly, but there was pride in her manner too.

"X" faced Gosseyn, peering at him from under the dome that covered his head. He said, "Gosseyn, you've put us into a dilemma. We're geared for action on a scale not seen since the third world war. We have been assigned nine thousand spaceships, forty million men, gigantic munitions factories, yet this is but a fraction of the military power of the greatest empire that ever was. Gosseyn, *we can't lose.*"

He paused, then went on, "Nevertheless, we prefer to play safe. We'd like to invite you, the unknown quantity,

91

to join us as one of the top leaders in the solar system."
He shrugged. "But you can understand that it would be
useless even to begin such a relationship if you turned out
to be unwilling to accept the realities of our position. We
have to kill, Gosseyn. We have to be ruthless. Killing con-
vinces people as nothing else will."

For a moment, Gosseyn thought he meant to kill
Amelia Prescott. A faintness seized him. And then he
realized that he had misunderstood.

"Kill!" he said blankly. "Kill whom?"

"About twenty million Venusians," answered "X." Sitting there in his wheel chair, he looked like a plastic nightmare beetle. "As you must know," he went on, "the only
difference between extinguishing the life in twenty human
nervous systems and twenty million is the effect on the
emotions of the survivors. Good propaganda should take
care of that."

Gosseyn felt as though he were standing at the bottom
of a well and sinking, sinking. "And what," he heard his
voice say hollowly out of the depths, "about the other two
hundred and twenty million inhabitants of Venus?"

"Terror!" said "X" in his G-string bass voice. "Merciless terror against those who resist. History teaches that
it has never been difficult to control the mass of a nation
once its head has been cut off. The head of Venus is a
very collective one, hence the large number of necessary
executions." He waved his plastic arm in an impatient
gesture. "All right, Gosseyn," he said curtly, "make up
your mind. We'll let you do a lot of the reorganizing, but
you must let us create the environment for it. Well, do we
make a deal?"

The question startled Gosseyn. He hadn't realized that
he was being given an argument which was supposed to
persuade him. It was a case of levels of abstraction in the
best null-A sense. These people were inured to the idea of
mass executions. He wasn't. The gap was unbridgeable because each side regarded the viewpoint of the other as
illogical. He felt the rigidity of his refusal creep through
his nervous system, through his body, until finally there
was only utter, complete, ultimate positivity. He said in a
quiet yet ringing voice, "No, Mr. 'X'. No deal. And may all

of you burn in an early Christian hell for even thinking of such murder."

"Thorson," said "X" steadily, "kill her!"

Gosseyn said blankly, "What?"

Then he dragged his four guards half a dozen feet before they held him. When he could see again, Amelia Prescott was still smiling. She did not struggle as Thorson jabbed a syringe into her arm just above the elbow, but she fell like a stone. The giant caught her easily. "X" said, "You see, Gosseyn, we have an advantage over non-Aristotelians. They're disturbed by scruples. We merely want to win. Now, that little incident was designed to—"

He stopped. A surprised look twisted his face. He tumbled slowly forward to the floor. The hard plastic of his leg, arm, and body made a thumping sound on the marble as he sprawled full length on the floor. Behind him, Hardie, an equally bewildered look on his classic features, slumped to his knees, then sideways to the floor. The guards were falling, two of them tugging at their guns, then yielding limply to unconsciousness.

Thorson lowered the body of Amelia Prescott to the floor, and sank down beside it. Near them, Patricia Hardie dropped down to the floor with a thud. In every part of the room, his enemies lay around Gosseyn, looking very dead.

It was all quite incomprehensible.

XV

The feeling of paralysis slid from Gosseyn. He dived jerkily for the nearest guard, and came up gun in hand. He stood then, holding the gun tensely, watching for movement in any of the bodies. There was none. Everybody lay very still.

Gosseyn began hurriedly to disarm the guards. Whatever the reason for the opportunity that had come to him, there was no time to waste. The job finished, he paused, and once more stared at the strange scene. There were nine guards. They slumped on the floor, their bodies forming an odd pattern as if, like so many ninepins, they had all been tumbled with one shove. Gosseyn noted, without thinking about it, that Eldred Crang was not among those present. His gaze wandered swiftly over the remaining bodies, the two women and the three men. He thought, almost blankly, "I'm not grasping this as I ought. I've got to get out of here. Somebody may come."

He didn't budge. There was another, a mighty thought in his mind: Were they really dead? That thought sent him plunging beside "X." Unthinking, he placed a hand on the plastic cage that supported "X"s middle. The fleshless smoothness of it made him jerk his hand away in abrupt repulsion. It was hard to think of the fellow as human. He forced himself to bend near the face and listen. A slow, rhythmic warmth bathed his ear. Gosseyn straightened. "X" was alive. They must all be alive.

He was about to climb to his feet when a sound at one of the doors froze him briefly where he was. Then, gun pointed, he flattened himself to the floor. As he lay there, eyes slitted, he cursed himself for having delayed. He could have been hundreds of feet away by this time.

The door opened and John Prescott came in.

Gosseyn got up, trembling from the reaction. Prescott grinned at him nervously. "Aren't you glad you took that antidote?" he said. "I put Drae powder in the air-conditioning machine, and you're the only one who—" He broke off. "What's wrong? Am I too late?"

It was a fast diagnosis. By accident, Gosseyn's gaze had touched Amelia Prescott's still body, where it lay on the floor near the huge Thorson. And memory had flooded through him. He said grimly, "Prescott, your wife had something injected into her arm before the others were affected by the powder. It was supposed to kill her. Better examine her."

There was time for examinations, now that the strange unconsciousness of these people had been explained. If the air-conditioning system had spread the anesthetic, then this scene of silent, slumped bodies would be repeated in every room. The only danger now was that somebody would come in from outside. Gosseyn watched as the Venusian listened briefly at his wife's heart, then took a little bottle out of his pocket. The bottle stopper had a syringe attached to it. Prescott pressed the needle into her thigh and looked up.

"That contains fluorescine," he explained. "If she's alive, her lips will turn greenish in about a minute."

After two minutes, the woman's lips remained pale and dead. The man stood up and looked around him curiously. And the odd thing, then, was that Gosseyn had no premonition. He watched the Venusian walk stiffly over to the pile of guns and carefully select two guns. That was the dominating impression, the care with which the man examined his weapons.

What followed was too swift for interference. Prescott walked over and put a bullet through "X"'s right eye. Blood spread over the man's face like a small, vivid fire. Prescott whirled. Shoving the gun against Hardie's forehead, he fired again. He ran down the line of guards then, body bent low, firing with both guns. He was twisting toward Thorson when he stopped. A bewildered look came into his face. The astounded Gosseyn caught him there and tore the automatics out of his hands.

"You incredible fool!" Gosseyn shouted. "Do you realize what you've done?"

An hour later, when they abandoned their stolen car deep in the fog-bound city, and the night around them was like a pall of gray-black smoke, they heard the first roaring of the news from a public-address speaker.

"Stand by for an important announcement from the President's palace!"

That was one voice. Another, sterner voice came on.

"It is my sad duty to announce that President Michael Hardie was assassinated this evening by a man known as Gilbert Gosseyn, an agent of the Games Machine. The immensity of the plot against the people of Earth is only beginning to be apparent. Gosseyn, whose escape was assisted by so-called Venusian detectives, is tonight the object of the greatest manhunt in recent history. All law-abiding citizens are ordered to remain at home. Anyone found on the streets will have only himself to blame if he is roughly handled. *Stay at home.*"

It was the mention of the Machine that brought to Gosseyn realization of the full implications of that hasty killing. The reference to him as its agent, and the attempt to tie in Venusian detectives—it was the first public attack against the sacred symbols of null-A that he had ever heard. Here was the declaration of war.

The fog wisped around them as they stood there. It was so thick Gosseyn could see Prescott two feet away as a shadow only. Radar, of course, could penetrate the fog as if it did not exist, but that would require instruments and the machines to transport them. A radar searchlight could silhouette them instantly, but it would have to be pointed at them first. In such a fog on such a night, bad luck could destroy him; otherwise he was safe. For the first time since events had seized hold of him, he was free to carry out his own purposes. Free, that is, with one limitation.

He turned to stare at Prescott, still the unknown factor. Recriminations for what had happend were, of course, useless. But even in this dark, miasmic night, it was difficult to know what to do with the man. Prescott had helped him to escape. Prescott knew much that could be valuable to him. Not now, not tonight. Now he had another, more urgent purpose. But in the long run Prescott might be very important to him.

If possible, he must try to keep this galactic convert to null-A as a companion. Swiftly, Gosseyn explained what was in his mind.

"A psychiatrist—and it can't be anyone I've contacted before—is obviously the first man on my list. There just isn't anything as important as finding out what in my brain has frightened everybody."

"But," protested Prescott, "he'll be under group protection."

Gosseyn smiled tolerantly into the night. He was physically and mentally at ease, conscious of his absolute superiority to his environment. "Prescott," he said, "I've been in this jam quite a while now. I've been like a bewildered child, timidly following other people's orders. I've told you, for instance, how I allowed the Machine to persuade me to be recaptured."

"Yes."

"I've been trying," Gosseyn went on, "to account for my easy acquiescence to such outside advice. And I think now it was because, way in the back of my mind, there's

96

been a desire to ease out from under all this and let somebody else take over the whole burden, or at least a part of it. I was so unwilling to recognize that I was *in* this affair as deep as I could go—so unwilling that the first thing I did was to get myself killed.

"Frankly," he finished, "I'm counting on that Drae powder of yours to disorganize any group protective system now organized. But first, I want you to buy a map of the city, then we'll look up the home adress of Dr. Lauren Kair. If he's not available, I'll accept anybody but Dr. David Lester Enright, with whom I once made an appointment."

Prescott said, "I'll be back in ten minutes."

Gosseyn spoke without rancor. "Oh, no, you won't." He explained gently, "We're in this together, each the guard of the other. I'll go into the drugstore behind you and look up Dr. Kair's address while you buy the map."

Doctor Kair's house gleamed whitely in the light from a corner lamp and from two dim globes that cast a pale radiance around their base, presumably indicating that the family was home. They vaulted the fence like wraiths. As they paused in the shadows of shrubbery, Prescott whispered, "Are you sure Dr. Kair is the man you want to see?"

"Yes," said Gosseyn. He was about to leave it at that, when the thought came that the author of *The Egotist on Non-Aristotelian Venus* deserved better. He added, "He's written some books."

It was a very Aristotelian way of putting it, but he was intent now. The house of Dr. Kair, and Dr. Kair himself, offered a unique problem. Here was a residence so protected against intruders by a group system that not even the most skillful gangs operating during the policeless period would dare to try to break in. The method of entry had to be aboveboard and not too involved, with a safe method of escape if the protective system was set in play. Gosseyn whispered, "This Drae powder you used—it affects the brain?"

"Instantly. It works on the nerves in the upper nostril cavities, thus making a direct path to the brain. One whiff is usually enough."

Gosseyn nodded, then turned his attention back to Dr.

97

Kair's house. In minutes, if nothing went wrong, a great semanticist, specializing in the human brain, would be questioning, examining, and diagnosing his brain. *His* brain, the existence of which had drawn Hardie and "X" into a vortex of events and brought about their death. Nothing mattered so much as finding out the why and how of this strange brain of his.

Gosseyn whispered his plan. Prescott would go to the door and identify himself as a Venusian. Undoubtedly, before admitting him, Dr. Kair would sound the group warning, placing his neighbors on the alert. But that was unimportant. The Drae powder would take care of an emergency.

Gosseyn asked, "How much of the powder would you use?"

"A pinch—one capsule. I put eight capsules into the air system at the palace, about a teaspoonful. It's very potent, but the antidote we took will still protect us." He added, "I'd better be ringing that doorbell."

Half a minute later, he was doing just that.

The fog drifted in through the open door with them. By agreement, they left the door partly open. It brought the night, and the safety of the night, closer. For Gosseyn, who was satisfied now with nothing less than every thinkable precaution, that unclosed door was the difference between ease and unease.

Dr. Kair was a tall, huskily built man of fifty, with a smooth, strongly jowled face. As Gosseyn came in, the doctor looked at him curiously with a pair of the most piercing gray eyes Gosseyn had ever seen. Gosseyn bore the scrutiny quietly. He knew better than to rush this early confidence-building stage. Minutes spent now might save hours later.

The psychiatrist wasted no time. As soon as Gosseyn had explained his purpose, he disappeared into his den and emerged again almost immediately carrying a small lie detector.

"Mr. Gosseyn," he said, "no Venusian or advanced null-A will accept for a moment the astonishing press and radio statements issued this evening by the government information bureau about President Hardie's assassination. In all my life I have never heard or seen anything so calculated to arouse the emotions of the ignorant and of the great mass of the half educated. Not since the dark ages of the mind has such an attempt been made to appeal to the mob spirit, and the final evidence of their venality is their accusation against Venusians and against the Machine. There is unquestionably an ulterior motive behind those statements, and that, in itself, entitles you to a hearing before all just men." He broke off. "You are prepared to face a lie detector?"

"Anything, sir," Gosseyn said, "so long as I do not have to lose consciousness. I'm sure you can understand the reason for that."

The doctor could. And in all the tests that followed, there was not an instant when Gosseyn did not have his hands and his mind free. All the tests! There were dozens; there were scores. For those involving machines, the doctor's laboratory-den, just off the center hall, was ideally located. With two exceptions, all the instruments could be moved to a chair from which Gosseyn could look slantwise through the den door at the partly open outer door.

Some of the machines glowed at him with hot electronic eyes that warmed his skin and dazzled him. Others were as bright as burnished metal, but cold and unfeelable. Still others showed no visible lights, yet buzzed or hummed or throbbed with power as their unhuman senses examined him. As test followed test, Gosseyn told his story.

His account was interrupted three times, twice when he had to hold still while ultra-sensitive rays examined the nature of the cells in his extra brain, and finally when Dr. Kair exclaimed sharply, "Then you did not yourself kill any of these men?"

Prescott looked up at the question. "No, I was the one who did that." He laughed grimly. "As you've guessed from what Gosseyn has said, I'm a person who had to choose between null-A and my position. I'll have to plead temporary insanity if I'm ever brought to trial."

Dr. Kair gazed at him soberly. "No plea of insanity," he said, "has ever been accepted from a null-A. You'll have to think of a better story that that."

"Story!" thought Gosseyn, and looked at Prescott—for the first time really looked at him.

The man's eyes were ever so slightly narrowed, watching him. One of his hands moved casually toward the gun in his right-hand coat pocket. It must have been an unconscious action; he couldn't really have expected to succeed, because Gosseyn beat him easily to the draw.

"I would say," said Gosseyn quietly a moment later, after they had disarmed the man, "that the house is surrounded."

XVI

The human nervous system is structurally of inconceivable complexity. It is estimated that there are in the human brain about twelve thousand millions of nerve cells or neurons, and more than half of these are in the cerebral cortex. Were we to consider a million cortical nerve cells connected with one another in groups of only two neurons each and compute the possible combinations, we would find the number of possible interneuronic connection-patterns to be represented by ten to the power of two million, seven hundred, and eighty-three thousand. For comparison . . . probably the whole sidereal universe does not contain more than ten to the power of sixty-six atoms.

A.K.

The light that poked through the long crack made by the partly open outer door must now temporarily be their shield. So long as the door remained as it was, the watchers outside would see a blurred shaft of brightness and all would seem well to them. There would, of course, be a limit to their patience and gullibility.

They tied Prescott hand and foot, and they gagged him, all with a swiftness that did not shrink from rough handling. Then they talked over the limitations of their temporary safety.

"He hasn't been outside," Gosseyn pointed out soberly. "But he must have established contact in some way."

Dr. Kair said, "I don't think we should let that bother us just now."

"Eh?"

The doctor's face was calm, his eyes grave. "What I've discovered about you," he said, "comes first." His tone grew more urgent. "You don't seem to realize, Gosseyn, that you're the important person in all this. There just isn't anything that matters so much, and we've got to take all the attendant risks."

It took time to really accept that, time to assemble his powers of concentration, and to lock the outside danger into a separate compartment of his mind and leave it there. It even took time to realize that he could listen to the most important information of his individual universe, and simultaneously carry on vital work.

"What you have in your head," the psychiatrist began, "is not an extra brain in the sense that you now have a higher intelligence potential. That isn't possible. The human brain that created the Games Machine and similar electronic and mechanical organisms has not even theoretically an intellectual equal in the universe. People sometimes think that the electronic brain system of the Machine constitutes a development superior to that of man. They marvel at the Machine's capacity to handle twenty-five thousand individuals at once, but actually it can do so only because twenty-five thousand electronic brains were set up in intricate series for just that purpose. And besides, these operations are all of a routine nature.

"That is not to say that the Machine cannot think creatively. It is located over a multimetal mine, which is completely under its control. It has laboratories, where robots work under its direction. It is capable of manufacturing tools, and does all its own replacement and repair work. It has a virtually inexhaustible source of atomic energy. The Machine, in short, is self-sufficient and superlatively intelligent, but it has limitations. These limitations were implanted from the beginning, and consist of three broadly based directives.

"It must operate the games fairly, within the framework of the laws laid down long ago by the Institute of General Semantics. It must protect the development of null-A in the broadest sense. It can kill human beings only when they directly attack it."

Gosseyn was searching Prescott. No detail of the man's clothing escaped his probing fingers. The pockets yielded

101

a pistol and two blasters, extra ammunition, a box of Drae powder capsules, a packet of antidote pills, and a pocketbook. He didn't stop with the pockets, but examined the cloth itself. The material was plastic, of the kind that was worn a few times and then discarded.

It was on the side of the heel of the right shoe that he found the printed instrument. It was an electronic locator device made of the same plastic as the shoe, and recognizable only by the pattern of wires that had been printed from a photographically reduced cut. Gosseyn sighed as he discovered it. It must have been by the use of such a device that Patricia Hardie had been able to run into his arms that first day, pretending she needed protection. He hadn't had time, then, to find out how he had been located. It was good to know. Explanations made the mind easy, took a score of tiny strains off the nervous system, and released the body from the thrall of negative excitations for more positive activity. It was easier, suddenly, to listen to the psychologist.

The doctor, too, had been combining activity with conversation. From his very first word, he had started packing the test material into a leather case. Photographs and notes went in the case. He opened machines and removed recording tubes, wires, screens, rolls of film, ribbons of autotype paper, and special sensitive sound and light tracks. Almost every item, before he packed it, was briefly interpreted.

"This proves the new brain is not cortical material . . . and this . . . and this . . . and this . . . that the cells are not thalamic . . . memory . . . association. Here are some of the main channels by which it is connected to the rest of the brain. . . . No indication that any impulses have flowed to or from the new gray matter."

He looked up finally. "The evidence shows, Gosseyn, that what you have resembles not so much a brain as the great control systems in the solar plexus and the spine. Only it is the most compact setup of controls that I have ever seen. The number of cells involved is equal to about a third of the total now in your brain. You've got enough control apparatus in your head to direct atomic and electronic operations in the microcosm, and there just aren't enough objects in the macrocosm to ever engage the full potential control power of the automatic switches and relays now in your brain."

Gosseyn hadn't intended to interrupt. But he couldn't help himself. "Is there any possibility," he said in a strained voice, "that I can learn to integrate that new brain *during the next hour?*"

The answer was a grave shake of the head. "Not in an hour, or a day, or a week. Have you ever heard of George, the boy who lived with the animals?

"George, a two-year-old baby boy, wandered off into the wilderness of foothills and brush behind his parents' farm. Somehow, he fumbled his way into the lair of a renegade female dog which had just given birth to a litter of pups. Most of the pups died, and the wretched bitch, heavy with milk, its ferocity restrained by dimly remembered human training, permitted the child to feed.

"Later, it hunted food for him, but hunger must have come often, because ants, worms, beetles, anything that moved and had life, were found to be part of the boy's diet when he was captured at the age of eleven, a sullen, ferocious animal, as wild as the pack of dogs whose leader he had become. His early history was pieced together from his actions and habits.

"Grunts, narls, growls, and a very passable bark—that was his language. Sociologists and psychologists realized the opportunity he represented, and failed hopelessly in their efforts to educate him. Five years after his capture, he had been taught to set up alphabet blocks, spelling out his name and the names of a few other objects. His aspect at this stage remained bestial. His eyes glowed with easy hatred. He descended frequently and with great agility to all fours, and, even after half a decade, his forest lore was astounding. The tracks of animals, even if hours old, could set him into such a state of excitement that he would jump up and down and whine with eagerness.

"He died at the age of twenty-three, still an animal, a wizened creature-boy looking hardly human in the bed of his padded cell. A post mortem revealed that his cortex had not developed fully, but that it existed in sufficient size to have justified belief that it might have been made to function."

Dr. Kair ended, "We could have made George human

now with what we know about the brain, but you will agree, I think, that your case and his are similar, with one difference—*your start as a human being.*"

Gosseyn was silent. For the first time, the problem of his extra brain had been clearly defined in the only possible rational way—by analysis and comparison. Until this moment his picture of it had been vague and idealistic, disturbing only because the new brain had shown no activity, no reactions whatever. But always, through the blur of his visualizations, hope had blazed. It had given him a measure of arrogance and of strength in the harder moments of his brief career as a potential savior of civilization. And somewhere inside his skin, permeating possibly his entire nervous system, he had felt pride that he was more than a man. That would remain, of course. It was human to be proud of physical or mental attributes that had come by chance. But as for the rest, as far as further development was concerned, it would undoubtedly take time.

The psychiatrist said, "If you are a true mutation, the man after man, and should it come down to a choice between saving you and letting this galactic army assault a peaceful civilization, then you may be sure that I shall choose you. And they"—he smiled grimly—"shall have their opportunity to test whether null-A can be destroyed by a first adversity."

"But the Venusians don't know." Gosseyn found his voice. "They don't even suspect."

"That," said Dr. Kair, "underlines with very special emphasis what our next move must be. Our future depends on whether or not we can escape from this house before dawn. And that"—he stood up with astonishingly youthful litheness—"brings us right back to our friend on the couch."

It was easy to think again of urgent and deadly danger.

XVII

We copy animals in our nervous processes. . . . In man such nervous reactions lead to non-survival, pathological states of general infantilism, infantile private and public behavior. . . . And the more technically developed a nation or race is, the more cruel, ruthless, predatory, and commercialized its systems tend to become . . . all because we continue to think like animals and have not learned how to think consistently like human beings.

A.K.

John Prescott, galactic agent. That much identification was admissible. The man lay on the couch and his eyes watched them. His blond hair seemed curiously whitish in the strong light. The faintest sneer lurked in the crinkles of his lips, in spite of the slightly bulging gag inside his mouth.

Gosseyn said with revulsion, "You know, there is something horrible here. This man allowed his wife to be murdered as a mere incident in a campaign to convince me of his *bona fides.* What took me in was that he had once been a partial believer in the null-A philosophy. I took it for granted, also, that his killing of 'X' and Hardie first was pure chance. But I recall now that he paused before he reached Thorson and gave me time to disarm him. In other words, he killed the two Earth men who had been used as a front by the galactic empire, which leaves only galactic people in control of the Earth government."

Gosseyn closed his eyes. "Just a moment," he said, "I'm thinking of something. The games. Weren't this year's games supposed to produce a successor to President Hardie?" He opened his eyes. "Who's ahead so far? Who's leading?"

Kair shrugged. "A man called Thorson." He stopped and blinked. "You know," he said slowly, "I didn't connect the name when you mentioned it. But there you have your answer."

Gosseyn said nothing. There was a thought in his mind that chilled him. It had very little to do with the fact that Jim Thorson, personal representative of a galactic emperor, would be the next president of Earth. The thought had to do with the Machine. It had outlived its usefulness. It would never again be trustworthy, now that it had proved vulnerable.

It was hard to imagine Earth without the Games Machine.

Beside him, Dr. Kair said gently, "All this is unimportant now. We have our own problem. As I see it, one of us must impersonate Prescott and go outside to assess the situation."

Gosseyn drew a deep, slow breath, and was himself. He said quickly, "What about your wife? Is she here? I've been intending to ask. And children. Any children?"

"Three but not here. Venusian-born children cannot visit Earth until they're eighteen. At the moment my wife is with them in New Chicago, Venus."

They smiled at each other, the doctor looking gleeful. He had a right to be. The two men were alone with their great problem: one, the doctor, of great attainment in his field; the other—well, the other had still to prove himself.

They decided without argument that Dr. Kair would go out to contact the gang's agents. His white hair and his build gave him an appearance roughly similar to that of Prescott. It should suffice in the dark. Prescott's shoes, while a little too long and half a size too narrow, fitted Kair. It seemed wise to wear the shoes that contained the locator. Imitating Prescott's voice was comparatively easy. Like all trained speakers, like all Venusians, the psychiatrist had full control of the resonance chambers in his body and head. With a recent memory of Prescott's voice and with Gosseyn there to check on the subtleties of tone, he had the imitation pat in three minutes, including an identifiable whisper.

"And now," said Gosseyn in a steely voice, "we'll find out from the gentleman himself the details of his arrangements with his friends outside."

He bent down and removed the gag. The disgust he felt must have been in his manner, or perhaps Prescott was persuaded by a knowledge of what he would have done to secure information under similar circumstances. Whatever the reason, he said without prompting, "I have no objection to telling you that there are a dozen men outside, and they have orders to follow you, not arrest you. I was supposed to go out about now, to let them know that everything was all right. The all-clear word is 'Venus.'"

Gosseyn nodded to the psychiatrist. "All right, Doctor,"

he said. "I'll expect you back in five minutes. If you're not, I'll suppress my squeamishness and put a bullet through Prescott's head."

The doctor laughed without humor. "Maybe it would be just as well if I stayed out six or seven minutes."

His laughter faded as he reached the door. The door moved slightly when he slipped through the opening. And then he was gone into the night and the fog.

Gosseyn glanced at his watch. "It is now ten minutes after four," he said to Prescott, and drew his gun.

A tiny bead of perspiration started a path down Prescott's cheek. It gave Gosseyn an idea. He looked again at his watch. The second hand, which had been at ten, was now at forty-five. Thirty-five seconds had passed. "One minute," said Gosseyn.

Physiological time was a flux of irreversible changes of the tissues and cells. But inward time depended on the human system, on variable circumstances, and on each individual. It changed under stress. Duration was as firmly wedded to man and his momentary emotions as life was to the nervous system. The second hand was twitching toward the ten, completing its first round. Accordingly, one minute had actually passed since the departure of Dr. Kair.

"Two minutes," said Gosseyn in an implacable tone.

Prescott said in a low, harsh voice, "Unless Kair is a fool he should be back in five minutes, but the contact man out there is a talkative idiot. Take that into account, and don't be too hasty."

By the time a minute and a half had gone by, Prescott was sweating profusely. "Three minutes," said Gosseyn.

Prescott protested, "I told you the truth. Why shouldn't I? You can't escape our dragnet for long. One week, two weeks, three weeks—what does it matter? After listening to Kair, it's clear to me that your chance of gaining control of that extra part of your mind is almost zero. That's what we wanted to find out."

It was curious, listening to the man talk and at the same time picturing Dr. Kair out in the fog of that pre-dawn night. His watch said that the psychiatrist had been gone only two minutes.

"Four minutes!" said Gosseyn.

It startled him a little. If a weak link was going to snap in Prescott's mind, it would have to be soon now. He leaned forward, expectant, his questions quivering on the tip of his tongue.

"Another reason I told the truth," Prescott babbled, "is that I am no longer convinced even a superman could interfere with the interplanetary operations which are now about to be launched. The organization has been overcautious in your case."

Gosseyn's watch showed twelve and one half minutes after four. According to the accelerated time sense working on Prescott's nervous system, the five minutes allotted for Dr. Kair's absence was up. It was too fast, it seemed to Gosseyn. By telescoping time in half, he hadn't given Prescott the opportunity to get really upset. It was too late to slow down. If the man was going to break, now was the time.

"The five minutes are up," he said decisively. He raised the gun. Prescott's face was a strange, livid color. Gosseyn added savagely, "I'm going to give you one more minute, Prescott. And if you haven't started talking then, or if Kair isn't back, you're through. What I want to know is, where did 'X' or the gang get the instrument they use to corrupt the Games Machine? And where is that instrument now?"

The words spoken, he glanced at his watch to emphasize the time limit. He stared, startled, and briefly forgot his purpose with Prescott. The time was fourteen minutes after four. Four minutes gone! He had an empty feeling, a qualm, the first shocked thought that Dr. Kair had been gone a long time. He saw that Prescott was gray, and that steadied his own nerves. Prescott said in a curious uneven tone, "The Distorter is in Patricia Hardie's apartment. We built it in to look like a part of one wall."

The man looked on the verge of collapse. And his story had the sound of truth. The "Distorter"—the very naming of it was a partial verification—*had* to be located near the Machine, and they would obviously try to conceal it. Why not in Patricia Hardie's room? Gosseyn suppressed an impulse to get the lie detector. Suppressed it because he had Prescott on the run, and the introduction of a machine might be fatal. But he couldn't prevent himself from taking another glance at his watch. It was 4:15 A.M. Gosseyn glared at the door. Time was calling his bluff. He began to understand the pressure Prescott had endured. With an effort he forced his attention back to the man.

"Where," he urged, "did you get the 'Distorter'?"

"Thorson brought it. It's being used illegally, since its use is forbidden by the League except for transport, and—"

A sound at the door silenced him. He relaxed with a sick grin as Dr. Kair came in, breathless.

"No time to waste," said the doctor. "It's getting light outside, and the fog is beginning to clear. I told them we were leaving right away. Come on."

He snatched up the leather case containing the test material about Gosseyn's brain. Gosseyn stopped him long enough for them to gag Prescott, long enough for him to have time to think, and say, "But where are we going?"

Kair was as gleeful as a boy who has tasted adventure. "Why, we're taking my private roboplane, of course. We're going to act just as if we're not being watched. As to *where* we're going, I'm sure you don't expect me to mention that in front of Mr. Prescott, do you? Particularly since I'm going to drop his shoes, with the locator device in them, before we're clear of the city."

In five minutes they were in the air. Gosseyn looked out into the pressing fog and felt the exultation gathering in him.

They were actually getting away.

XVIII

Gosseyn sank deeper into his seat in the roboplane and glanced at Dr. Kair. The psychiatrist's eyes were still open, but he looked very sleepy. Gosseyn said, "Doctor, what is Venus like—the cities, I mean?"

The doctor rolled his head sideways to look at Gosseyn, but did not move his body.

"Oh, much like Earth cities, but suited to the perpetually mild climate. Because of the high clouds it never gets too hot. And it never rains except in the mountains. But every night on the great verdant plains, there's a heavy dew. And I mean heavy enough to look after all the luxuriant growth. Is that what you're getting at?"

It wasn't. "I mean the science." Gosseyn frowned. "Is it different? Is it superior?"

"Not one whit. Everything ever discovered on Venus is immediately introduced on Earth. As a matter of fact, research on Earth is ahead of Venus on some things. Why shouldn't it be? There are more people here, and specialization makes it possible for minds of middling intelligence—even unsane minds—to invent and discover."

"I see." Gosseyn was intent now. "Tell me, then. From your knowledge of Earth and Venusian science, what is the explanation for two bodies and the same personality?"

"I intended to think about that in the morning," said Dr. Kair wearily.

"Think about it now." Gosseyn was persistent. "Is there any explanation on the basis of solar science?"

"None that I know of." The psychiatrist was frowning. "There's no question, Gosseyn. You've hit at the heart of this situation. Who discovered such absolutely radical processes? I have no doubt there have been some potent biological experiments undertaken in the solar system by semantically trained biologists. But two bodies and a new brain!"

"Notice," said Gosseyn softly, "both sides have something. The miracle of my strange immortality was a product of somebody who opposes the group that owns the Distorter. And yet, Doctor, my side—our side—is afraid. It must be. If it had comparable strength, it wouldn't play this hidden game."

"Hm-m, you seem to have something there."

Gosseyn persisted, "Doctor, if you were a human being powerful enough to make decisions of planetary importance on your own, what would you do if you discovered that a galactic empire was organizing to seize an entire sun system?"

The older man snorted. "I'd rouse the people. The strength of null-A has yet to be tested in battle, but I have an idea it will show up well."

Several minutes passed before Gosseyn spoke again. "Where are we going, Doctor?"

Dr. Kair perked up for the first time. "There's a

cabin," he said, "on an isolated shore of Lake Superior where I stayed a couple of months three years ago. It seemed such an ideal place for quiet thought and research that I bought the place. And then never went back, somehow." He smiled wryly. "I'm pretty sure we'll be safe there for a while."

Gosseyn said, "Oh!"

He sat there estimating the time that had passed since their flight began. He decided half an hour had gone by. Not bad, in a way. A man who could in thirty minutes realize that the enticing easy path was not for him had come a long distance toward domination of his environment. It *was* enticing to think of lying for hours on some sandy beach, with nothing to do but take mind exercises, in a leisurely fashion, under the guidance of a great scientist. The one flaw in the picture was a rather tremendous one. It wouldn't be like that at all.

He pictured Dr. Kair's cabin hideout, There would be a village near by, and perhaps some farms and fishermen's homes. Three years before, with a clear conscience, intent on his own purposes, the psychiatrist would have been almost unaware of these addenda to his surroundings. He had probably caught up on his reading and gone for meditative walks on lonely shores, and the occasional habitant whom he met would have been a person seen but not really considered. That didn't mean that the doctor himself would have been unremarked. And the chances of two men coming to that cabin immediately after the assassination of Hardie and not being closely observed were—well, they were zero.

Gosseyn sighed. For him there could be no time for settling down on some lake-shore pasture, there to vegetate while the inhabited worlds of the solar system rocked under the impact of invading armies. He stole another look at the doctor. The man's shaggy head was drooped against the back of his seat; his eyes were closed. His chest rose and fell with regularity. Softly, Gosseyn called, "Doctor!"

The sleeper did not sitr.

Gosseyn waited a minute, then slipped to the controls. He set them to make a wide half circle, and head back in the direction from which they had come. He returned to his seat, took out his notebook, and wrote:

Dear Doctor:

Sorry to leave you like this, but if you were awake we'd probably only argue. I am very anxious to undergo mind training, but there are urgent things to do first. Watch the evening paper personals. Look for an ad signed by "Guest." If answer is necessary, sign yourself "Careless."

He stuck the note into the controls and then strapped on one of the ingravity parachutes. Twenty minutes later, the atomic light of the Machine showed through the fog. Once more, Gosseyn set the controls for a wide half circle, so that the plane would return to its original course.

He waited till the blazing beacon of the Games Machine was like a raging fire below him, then slightly behind. He saw the vaguely shaped buildings of the presidential residence just ahead. When the plane was almost over the palace, he pulled the trigger of the exit door.

Instantly he was falling through the foggy darkness.

XIX

Even Leibnitz formulated the postulate of continuity, of infinitely near action, as a general principle, and could not for this reason become reconciled to Newton's Law of Gravitation, which entails action at a distance.

H.W.

The ingravity parachute was in its entirety a product of purest null-A thinking. Its discoverer had actually sat down and consciously and deliberately worked out the mathematical principles involved; then he had superintended the construction of the first plates. It did its work within the limitations of that law of gravity which said that it is easier for two objects in space to fall toward each other than away from each other, with the smaller of the two doing most of the actual falling. Only an applied force could change this tendency, and applied forces had tendencies of their own that usually included bulkiness, weight, and a capacity for being dangerous when used in close proximity to human beings. There were still Aristotelians around who had fuzzy ideas about making things "fall" upward, and who talked semantic rubbish about nothing being impossible. Non-Newtonian physics, the physics of the real world, recognized the urge of the two bodies to fall toward each other as an invariant of nature, and simply adjusted their nucleonic structures to slow the fall.

The ingravity parachute resembled a metal harness, with pads to protect the body where the pressure was greatest. It had power attachments, but they were for maneuvering sideways during the fall. The slowest rate of fall ever clocked was approximately five miles per hour, which meant that the device had an efficiency of slightly better than ninety per cent.

Accordingly, it rivaled the electric motor, the steam turbine, the atomic drive for spaceships, and the suction pump as a "perfect" machine. By pressing the proper power buttons, Gosseyn had no trouble landing squarely on the balcony that led into Patricia Hardie's apartment. He would have liked to pay the Games Machine a visit first, but that was out of the question. The Machine would be guarded like the crown jewels of olden days. But nobody would think of his coming back to the palace—he hoped!

He took the slight blow of the landing with bended knees and came up like a boxer, on his toes. The parachute was a zipper affair; one tug and he was out of it. He lowered it swiftly but quietly to the floor. And then he was at the French doors. The doors opened with a thin, sharp click. Gosseyn didn't worry about the sound.

His plan was based on speed and on a very clear memory of where Patricia Hardie's bed had been located. He had been undecided as to exactly how he should treat her. She might believe that he had killed her father; and here, now, on the scene, with the decision no longer to be postponed, he realized he had to take that possibility into account.

He pinned her down in the bed and put his hand over her mouth. He gagged her, tied her, then drew back and switched on the light. He looked down at her and said, "Sorry if I was rough with you."

He was sorry. But there was more behind the words

than that. As soon as he had located and rendered harmless the Distorter, he hoped to effect his escape from the palace with her help.

He saw that her eyes were fixed on a point behind him. Gosseyn whirled. From the doorway Eldred Crang said, "I wouldn't try anything."

His hazel eyes glowed with reflected light. He stood at ease, flanked by two men with blasters. Gosseyn put up his hands as Crang spoke again.

"It was very foolish of you, Gosseyn, to think an airplane could fly directly over the palace tonight. However, I have a surprise for you. Prescott was released a little while ago, and he called up. On the basis of his report, I have persuaded Thorson to let me handle you in my own way."

Gosseyn waited, but the first hope was on him. Crang, the secret null-A, had *persuaded* Thorson. He had taken it for granted that Crang's position was too difficult for him to show the slightest favor to him, and yet the man had dared to do so. Crang went on:

"It struck us some little while ago that whoever planted you on us that first time didn't care whether or not you were killed. In fact, we believe that after your extra brain was discovered it was intended that you be put to death. Promptly, you were brought onto the scene a second time, this time on Venus, to accomplish another limited objective. I won't tell you what it was, but I assure you that you accomplished it. Once more, however, the person behind you seemed unconcerned with your personal welfare. The conclusion is inescapable. There must be a third Gosseyn body waiting to come to life as soon as the second body is out of the way."

He smiled. His eyes shone like fire. "This man who is behind you, Gosseyn, has quite a problem. It is obvious that he would not dare to have two living bodies out at one time. For one thing, it would be too complicated; for another, it has dangerous possibilities of each body developing other duplicates of itself, with each duplicate as egotistical and powerful as the others. You can see where that might lead."

Crang shook his head slightly.

"Thorson argued that we should hold you prisoner, but I maintain that death or imprisonment are but facets of the same thing. And that either would be the signal for the appearance of Gosseyn III. We don't want that. And if we don't kill you, then no one else will except you yourself—or some other agent of the invisible chess player.

"Accordingly, we have decided to release you unconditionally, in the belief that you will protect yourself from harm."

He hadn't expected that. Just what he should hope for he couldn't decide. Not freedom. He had been trying to gauge the limitations of Crang's position, and even to wonder why Crang, a null-A supporter, would oppose the coming of Gosseyn III. The abrupt announcement, favorable from his own point of view, puzzling from Crang's, caught him by surprise.

"You're going to *what?*" said Gosseyn.

"The charges against you," said Crang in a precise voice, "are being dropped. All police stations are being notified to that effect. At this moment you are free. Nothing that you, with your undeveloped brain, can do matters to us. It is too late to interfere with our plans. You may tell anybody you please anything you please."

He turned. His manner was easy but not friendly. "Guards," he said, "take this man up to his apartment, see that he gets breakfast, and fit him with suitable street clothes. Let him remain in the palace till about nine o'clock, but he can leave earlier if he desires."

Gosseyn allowed himself to be led away. He dared not speak to Patricia and dared not thank Crang for fear that Thorson might be listening in. Day was bright though still misty over the city of the Machine as Gosseyn emerged into the open shortly after nine o'clock.

XX

Excitation rather than inhibition is important in correlation because from what has been said it appears that so far as is known, inhibition is not transmitted as such. The existence of inhibitory nervous correlation is, of course, a familiar fact, but in such cases the inhibitory effect is apparently produced not by transmission of an inhibitory change but by transmission of an excitation, and the mechanism of the final inhibitory effect is obscure.

C.M.C.

Out on the street, Gosseyn said softly to himself, "Somebody will be following me. Thorson won't just let me wander off into remoteness."

He was the only person who got on the bus at the head of the street. He watched the gray pavement slide away behind the machine. About two blocks to the rear was either a black or blue coupé; he couldn't be sure of the color. He sighed as it turned into a side street and disappeared from sight. A very fast car came from the far distance beyond the palace and raced past the bus, which was stopping for a woman. She paid him no attention, but he kept his surreptitious gaze on her until she got off after twenty blocks or so.

"Maybe," he decided, "they've guessed where I'm going—first the hotel, then the Games Machine."

At the hotel, where the first Gosseyn had left his possessions, including some two hundred dollars in paper money, the clerk said, "Sign here, please."

Gosseyn hadn't thought of that. He took the pen, a vision of jail looming up. He signed with a flourish, and then smiled to himself as he realized what an almost nerveless person he had become.

He watched the clerk disappear into a back room. Half a minute later the man emerged with a key.

"You know the way to the vault," he said.

Gosseyn did. But he was thinking, "Even my signature's the same, an automatic sameness." The explanation for such identity had better be good.

He spent ten minutes rummaging through the suitcases. It was the three suits he was interested in. He had, he remembered, set the thermostat on one of them at 66° Fahrenheit, whereas normal for him was 72.

As he had recalled, two of the readings were 72, one was 66. He took off the clothes that had been given him at the palace and put on one of his own suits. It fitted perfectly. Gosseyn sighed. In spite of everything, it was hard to accept the similarity between himself and a dead man.

He found his money where he had laid it, between the leaves of one of his books. He counted off seventy-five dollars in tens and fives, put the suitcases back in the vault, and returned the keys to the desk. Out on the street, a shout from an automatic newspaper dispenser brought remembrance of the wild announcements and accusations of the night before. The President's death made the expected huge headline, but the write-ups below had been toned down almost beyond recognition:

". . . Gosseyn exonerated. . . . A thorough investigation being made. . . . Administration officers admit many foolish statements given out immediately after murder. . . . Jim Thorson, leading presidential candidate in the games, asks . . . due process of law."

It was backing down with a vengeance. But it was clever, too—the easy cleverness of men with unlimited strength behind them. The seed of suspicion of Venus and the Machine had been planted. At the proper time it would be made to sprout.

There was a tiny item on the first page of the second section which interested Gosseyn. It read:

NO NEWS FROM VENUS
The Radio Exchange reports that
no contact could be established this
morning with Venus.

The report depressed Gosseyn. It drove home a reality that had been nibbling at the outer ramparts of his mind ever since he had left the palace. He was back in the depths, back with the five billion people who knew nothing except what they were told, back in darkness. Worse than that, he who had been keyed up by danger to actions that smacked of sheer melodrama in retrospect had had the danger taken from him. Imagine dropping on the palace on the night of the assassination of President Hardie. It was the act of a madman, certainly beyond the capacity of an ordinary law-abiding individual like Gilbert Gosseyn. Surely they would prevent him from getting in to see the Machine.

But nobody stopped him. The great avenues leading to

the Machine were almost deserted, which was not surprising on the twenty-ninth day of the games. More than ninety per cent of the competitors must have been eliminated by now, and their absence showed. Inside a cubbyhole of the type used for the early part of the games, Gosseyn picked up the metal contacts necesssary to establishing rapport and waited. After about half a minute, a voice spoke from the wall speaker in front of him.

"So that's the situation, is it? What are your plans?"

The question shocked Gosseyn. He had come for advice, even—he was loath to admit it—instructions. His own ideas about his future were so obscure that it was improper to call them plans.

"I've been caught off balance," he confessed. "After living on danger, the fear of death, and a sense of harrowing urgency, I have suddenly had the whole load lifted from my shoulders. I'm back in purgatory, with rooms to locate, a living to make, and all the wretched details of a low-income existence to attend to. My only plan is to talk to some of the professors at the Semantics Institute, and get in touch with Dr. Kair. Somehow, the Venusians have to be warned of their danger."

"The Venusians know," the Machine said. "They were attacked sixteen hours ago by five thousand spaceships and twenty-five million men. They—"

Gosseyn said, *"What?"*

"At this moment," said the Machine, "the great cities of Venus are in the hands of the conquerors. The first phase of the battle is accordingly over."

Limply, Gosseyn let go of the metal contact. There was dismay in him that completely overrode the enormous respect he had always had for the Machine.

"And you didn't warn them!" he raved. "Why, you incredible monster!"

"You have, I believe," said the Machine coolly, "heard of the Distorter. I can make no public statements while that instrument is focused on me."

Gosseyn, whose lips had been parted for another tirade, closed them and sat silent, as the Machine went on:

"An electronic system of brains is a very curious and limited structure. It works by a process of intermittent power flow. In this process the denial of power at the

118

proper split instants is as important as the flow during other split instants. The Distorter permits only movement of energy, not the hindrances or the variances. When it is focused on any part of me, the particular function to which it is attuned ceases to have inhibitions. In photo-electric cells, thyratrons, amplifiers, and in every part of my structure, the flow of energy becomes uniform and meaningless. My system of public communicators is constantly under this baneful influence."

"But you can talk to me as an individual. You *are!*"

"As an individual," said the Machine. "By concentrating all my powers I could tell three or four people the truth at any one time. Suppose I did. Suppose a few dozen individuals started to go around telling others by word of mouth that the Machine was accusing the government of chicanery. Before anybody really believed it, the gang would hear the reports and concentrate another Distorter on me. No, my friend, the world is too big, and the group can start more rumors in one hour than I could set going in a year. It must be a public broadcast on a planetary scale, or it means nothing."

"But," said Gosseyn blankly, "what are we going to do?"

"*I* can do nothing."

The accent on the pronoun was not lost on Gosseyn. "You mean, I can do something?"

"It all depends," said the Machine, "on how completely you understand that Crang's analysis of the situation was masterly."

Gosseyn threw his mind back to what Crang had said. All that nonsense about why they weren't going to kill him, and about—"Now, see here," he said loudly, "you don't really mean that I'm supposed to kill myself."

"I would have," said the Machine, "shot you the moment you came in here today if I had been able. But I can kill human beings only in self-defense. That is a permanent inhibition upon my powers."

Gosseyn, who had never thought of danger from the Machine, rasped, "But I don't understand. What's going on?"

The Machine's voice seemed to come from a long way off. "Your work is done," it said. "You have accomplished your purpose. Now you must give away to the third and greatest Gosseyn. It is possible," the cool voice went on, "that you could learn to integrate your extra brain in this body, given time. But there isn't time available. Accordingly, you must make way for Gosseyn III, whose brain will be integrated from the moment he comes to conscious life."

"But that's ridiculous," Gosseyn said jerkily. "I can't kill myself." He controlled himself with an effort. "Why can't this—this third Gosseyn come to life without my dying?"

"I don't know too much about the process," said the Machine. "Since I last saw you, I have been told that the death of one body is recorded on an electronic receiver, which then triggers the new body into consciousness. The mechanical part of the problem seems very simple, but the biological part sounds intricate."

"Who told you this?" Gosseyn asked tautly.

There was a pause, then a slot opened and a letter slid out of it. "I receive my instructions by mail," said the Machine matter of factly. "Your second body was delivered to me by truck, with that note attached."

Gosseyn picked up the sheet and unfolded it. A typewritten message had been printed on otherwise blank paper:

Ship body of Gosseyn II to Venus and have one of your roboplane agents deposit it in forest near Prescott home. When he leaves this residence, pick him up and set him down near Crang's tree home with instructions to surrender himself. Give him information about Venus, and take any necessary precautions.

The Machine said, "Nobody ever questions my shipments to Venus, so that was no problem."

Gosseyn reread the note, feeling faint. "But is this all you know?" he managed to say finally.

The Machine seemed to hesitate. "I have received one message since then, to the effect that the body of Gosseyn III will shortly be delivered to me."

Gosseyn was pale. "You're lying," he said harshly. "You're telling me that so that I'll have an incentive to kill myself."

He stopped. He was talking about the act, discussing it as if it was something to be argued. Whereas the reality was that it wasn't a matter of not killing himself because of this or that or the other. He wasn't killing himself—just like that. Without another word he turned and strode out of the cubbyhole, out of and away from the Machine.

All through that day he was a man torn by a mixture of amazement and despair. By evening the high fever of restlessness was beginning to recede. He felt tired and unhappy, but also much more thoughtful. The Machine had not even suggested that he try to get the Distorter, perhaps because it could not imagine him succeeding.

As he ate dinner he visualized how it might be done. Phone Patricia and make an appointment with her in her apartment. Surely he could persuade her to see him some time during the following day, without any of the others knowing about it. The attempt had to be made.

He phoned her as soon as he had eaten. There was a slight delay after he gave his name, and then her face came on the video plate. Her face lighted, but she said hurriedly, "I can't talk to you more than a minute. Where can we meet?"

When he told her she frowned at him, started to shake her head, and then stared at him thoughtfully. She said finally, slowly, "This sounds awfully risky to me, but I'm willing to take the chance if you are. One o'clock tomorrow, and the important thing is, don't run into Prescott or Thorson or Mr. Crang as you come in."

Gosseyn told her gravely that he would be careful, said good-by, and hung up. It was Prescott that he met.

XXI

A famous Victorian-era physicist said, "There's nothing for the next generation of physicists to do except measure the next decimal place." In the next generation . . . Planck developed the quantum theory that led to Bohr's atomic structure work. . . . Einstein's mathematics were proven out by some extremely delicate decimal place measuring. . . . Obviously, the next question is going to involve the next set of decimal places. Gravity is too little understood. So are magnetic field phenomena. . . . Sooner or later somebody will slip another decimal place, and the problem will be solved.

J.W.C., Jr.

Gosseyn walked up to the main entrance a few minutes before one o'clock. He was not alone. Men and women moved in and out of the great doors, and their presence threw a sort of fog around him, hiding him from close observation. There was, of course, the necessity of passing the guard office inside the entrance. Gosseyn peered into the glass wicket at the chunky individual who sat there.

"My name is Gosseyn. I have an appointment with Miss Patricia Hardie for one o'clock."

The man ran his finger down a list of names. Then he pressed a button. A long young man in uniform popped out of a door near the wicket. He took Gosseyn's brief case and led the way to an elevator, the doors of which were just opening. One of the three people who came out was Prescott. He stared at Gosseyn in surprise. His face darkened.

"What brings you back here?" he asked.

Gosseyn braced himself. There was nothing to do but make the best of the fantastically bad luck. He had a vague plan for such a meeting as this, but his heart sank like a lead weight as he said the words he had prepared: "I have an appointment with Crang."

"Eh? Why, I just left Crang. He didn't mention that he was seeing you."

Gosseyn remembered that Prescott didn't know that Crang was a null-A supporter. All things considered, that was very fortunate.

"He's giving me a few minutes," he said. "But maybe you've got some ideas on what I have to say."

Prescott stood, cold, watchful, suspicious, as Gosseyn described his visit to the Machine and how the Machine wanted him to kill himself so that a third Gosseyn might appear. He omitted what the Machine had told him of the attack on Venus, and finished darkly, "I've got to see that third body. I'm just enough of a null-A not to believe in the triplicate even after I've seen the duplicate. Imagine anybody expecting a person of my sanity training to blow out his brains." He shuddered involuntarily. "I'm looking for clues," he said. "I even thought of coming to talk with Thorson. Somehow"——he looked hard at the other——"after last night, I didn't think of you."

Prescott's countenance showed no hint of his reaction to the night before. He turned, started to walk away, then came back. He stood staring at Gosseyn. His manner remained coldly hostile, but his eyes were curious.

"As you've probably guessed," he said, "we're looking for other bodies of yours."

Gosseyn's impulse had been to get away from Prescott. Now he felt a chill. "Where have you looked?" he asked.

Prescott laughed harshly. "At first we had some pretty wild ideas. We made soundings from the air for caves, and we searched in out-of-way places. But now we've grown a little smarter."

"What do you mean?"

"The problem," Prescott continued, frowning, "is greatly complicated by a law of nature, of which you have probably never heard. The law is this: If two energies can be attuned on a twenty-decimal approximation of similarity, the greater will bridge the gap of space between them just as if there were no gap, although the juncture is accomplished at finite speeds."

"That," said Gosseyn, "sounds like pure Greek."

Prescott laughed, louder this time. "Think of it this way, then," he said. "How do you explain the fact that you have in your mind the details of what Gosseyn I did and thought? You must have been attuned, you and he; in fact, it is the only theoretically sure method of thought transmission—you have to do it with yourself. Anyway, it didn't matter where you were; his thoughts, *being alive,* would have been the stronger, and would have flashed to you wherever you were within the limits of reachable space. I won't define those limits."

He broke off. "We've even examined meteorites as far away as the rings of Saturn in the apparently mistaken belief that some of them might have been hollowed out and fitted up as incubators with Gilbert Gosseyns in various stages of growth. That will show you how seriously we—"

There was an interruption from a man in military uniform.

"Our car is waiting, Mr. Prescott. The ship leaves for Venus on the half hour."

"Be right with you, General."

He turned and started to follow the officer. Then he paused and came back. He said, "In a way we're curious to see this Gosseyn III. Since you will already have had cautious thoughts in that connection, I am not giving anything away when I say that we shall kill him, and that then there will be no reason for not killing you. I suggest, furthermore, that there *must* be an end somewhere to the total number of Gilbert Gosseyns."

He twisted away and, without looking back, walked to the door. There was a car waiting at the foot of the steps. Gosseyn saw him climb into it. In a few moments, Prescott would be thinking over the meeting. And somewhere along the line he would phone Crang, who would then have to take action.

Gosseyn could hardly stand still in the elevator. His plan to get hold of the Distorter intact was shattered by the accidental meeting, but he wasted no time after Patricia Hardie let him into her apartment. Even as she was murmuring something about how dangerous it was for him to come to the palace, he was tugging a cord out of the bottom of his brief case.

She was amazed when he started to tie her. She had a little automatic up the voluminous sleeve of her dress that she tried to get at. Gosseyn took it and shoved it in his pocket. When he had carried her, bound and gagged, into the bedroom and laid her on the bed, he said, "I'm sorry. But this is for your own good, in case somebody interrupts us."

He wasn't sorry. He was only in a hurry. He hurried into the living room for his brief case. The tools in it he tumbled onto the bed beside the girl. From the pile he snatched an atomic cutter and ran for the wall he had decided the previous night was the only one the Distorter could possibly be in.

The Distorter *must* be facing the Games Machine a third of a mile away. And whatever its form, it couldn't be too tiny. At six hundred yards, even a searchlight had to have power and size behind it to shine brightly. Gosseyn adjusted the atomic cutter to penetrate the wire which was underneath the plaster. He sheared an eight-foot square and with a jerk pulled the wall down. Trailing a shower of fine dust, he carried it and set it against the alcove wall. When he came back, there was the Distorter. It was about six feet high by four feet wide by one and a half thick. It was smaller than he had expected and it had no visible wires running from it. Gosseyn caught it between his hands and gave a tentative tug. It came up in his hands lightly. About fifty pounds, he estimated, as he carried it over near the bed and laid it, face upward, on the rug. He stared down at a mass of tiny protruding, glasslike tubes. Obviously an electronic device of some kind, one of the quantity of developments on an intricate variational theme that had begun several hundred years before. He snatched the atomic cutter from the bed and, whirling toward the Distorter, prepared to cut it into bits. As he bent over it, he paused, frowning, and looked at his watch. It was twenty-five minutes to two.

The fever of his urgency abated. Prescott's ship had departed for Venus and nothing had happened. He went over and gazed out of the French windows. The great sweep of lawn that led toward the Machine, spaced here and there with shrubs, was almost deserted. At uneven intervals, gardeners were stooping over flowers, performing the tasks of their profession. Beyond was the Machine, an enormous glittering mass surmounted by its quadrillion-candlepower beacon. It shouldn't take more than a few minutes to get the Distorter over there.

With abrupt decision, Gosseyn picked up Patricia Hardie's bedside phone and, when a girl's voice answered, said, "Give me the chief carpenter, please."

"I'll connect you with the Palace Works Superintendent," the operator said.

A moment later, a gruff voice muttered at Gosseyn, who explained what he wanted and hung up. He was quivering with excitement.

"It's got to work," he thought tautly. "Things like this always work when put through with boldness."

He hurriedly carried the Distorter into the living room. Then he closed the bedroom door. A short time later there was a pounding at the corridor door. Gosseyn unlocked the door and five men trooped in, three of them carrying lumber. Without pause these three fell to work and crated the Distorter. They had silent cutting machines, automatic screwdriving devices; in seven minutes, by Gosseyn's watch, they were finished. The two truckmen, who had so far done nothing, picked up the crate. One of them said, "We'll have this delivered in five minutes, mister."

Gosseyn closed and locked the door behind him, and then went into the bedroom. He didn't glance at the girl, but hurried to the French windows. In two minutes a truck with a narrow crate on it wheeled into view on the paved road a quarter of a mile away. It drove straight up to the Machine and disappeared into an overlapping fold of metal. Two minutes later it reappeared, empty.

Without a word, Gosseyn walked over and ungagged and unbound the girl. He was conscious of a vague dissatisfaction, an inexplicable sense of frustration.

XXII

> Who, then, is sane?
> (*Quisnam igitur sanus?*)
> Horace: *Satires, II*
> *circa* 25 B.C.

Patricia Hardie sat on the bed rubbing the circulation back into her arms. She didn't speak, simply sat there massaging, and looking at him, a faint smile curling her lips. The smile puzzled Gosseyn. He glanced at her sharply and saw that the smile was cynical, knowing.

"So you didn't succeed!" she said.

Gosseyn stared at her. She went on, "You were hoping you'd be killed when you came to the palace today, weren't you?"

Gosseyn parted his lips to say, "Don't be silly!" But he didn't say it. He was visualizing his tight-stomached approach to the palace, his successful accomplishment of his purpose, and then his disappointment. Surely, surely men could fool themselves. The girl's voice came again, stinging now. "That's the only reason you came to get the

Distorter. You know you've got to die and let Gosseyn III appear. And so you were hoping the attempt would land you in deadly danger."

He could see it clearly now. No sane man could commit suicide or let others kill him without resisting. And so his subconscious had tried to find a way out. "Do I believe," he wondered, "in Gosseyn III? I do." He felt stunned. Because he had told himself again and again that it was impossible. "Can I kill myself? Not yet! But there is a way. *There is a way.*"

Gosseyn turned from the girl without a word, and started for the door.

"Where are you going?" she called after him.

"Back to my hotel. You can reach me there any time." He paused at the door. He had nearly forgotten that she had a problem, too.

"Better get some plasterers up here to put that wall back in place. As for what else you should do, I'm assuming you know your position better than I, so I'll leave that up to you. Good-by, and good luck."

He went out of the door and down onto the boulevard. Downtown, he stopped in a drugstore and asked for a bottle of hypnotic drug.

"Starting to train early for next year's games, eh?" said the druggist.

"Something like that," Gosseyn replied shortly.

He went next to a voice-recording firm. "I'd like to rent one of your machines for a week for repeat recordings."

"Do you want the attachment to make your own recordings?"

"Yes."

"That will be four dollars and fifty cents, please."

At the hotel where he had his things, Gosseyn secured the key to his locker and took out the rest of his money; then he returned to the desk. "On the first day of the games," he said, "I was kicked out of this hotel because of a mix-up over my identity. Will you rent me a room now for a week?"

The clerk did not hesitate. The hotel must have been practically empty, after the great exodus from the city of people who had failed to win at the games. In two minutes a bellhop was leading Gosseyn up to a spacious room.

Gosseyn locked the door, made the recording he had planned, and put it on the player to repeat endlessly. Then he swallowed the hypnotic drug and lay down on the bed. "In twenty-four hours," he thought, "the effect will wear off, and then—" He put the glittering little automatic he had taken from Patricia Hardie on the table beside the bed.

It was not sleep that came then. It was a torpor, a heavy tiredness through which impressions filtered, particularly noise. One noise, one steady, whining sound—the sound of his voice on the recording he had made.

"I'm nobody. I'm not worth anything. Everybody hates me. What's the good of being alive? I'll never make anything of myself. No girl will ever marry me. I'm ruined . . . no hope . . . no money . . . kill myself . . .

"Everybody hates me . . . hates me . . . hates me . . ."

There were millions of unintegrated people who thought and thought things like that, without ever reaching the point of suicide. It was a matter of sustained intensity and of the awful unbalance that came to men who had tumbled from a height of integration into the depths of despair.

"What's the good of being alive? What's the good . . . no hope . . . kill myself!"

During the first hour, he had many intruding thoughts of his own. "This is silly! My brain is too stable for it ever to be affected by. . . . *No hope . . . Everybody hates me . . . I'm not worthy . . ."*

It was toward the end of the second hour that a thunderous roar began far away. It kept on and on, frequently rising to such a crescendo that the whining voice beside the bed was drowned out. At last the violent persistence of it wrung a dull, surprised recognition from Gosseyn. "Guns! Artillery fire! Have they started to attack Earth?"

He was conscious of horror. Without having any memory of deciding to get up, he *was* up. How tired he was! *"I'm not worthy . . . ruined . . . no hope . . . kill myself . . ."*

Wearily, he crawled across the floor to the window. He peered out at another building But the thunder of the guns was louder here, and more furious sounding. And it was coming from the direction of the Machine! For a mo-

128

ment of terrible fear the daze lifted from his mind. The Machine was being attacked!

"I'm nobody . . . Kill myself . . . Everybody hates me . . . What's the good of being alive?"

The Machine, with the Distorter in its possession and under control, must have started broadcasting warnings about the attack on Venus! And the gang was trying to destroy it.

Broadcasting! The hotel-room radio! Crawl toward it. How tired he was! *"Kill myself . . . No hope!"* He reached the radio finally, switched it on.

"Blasted . . . murderous . . . incredible . . criminal . " . . "

Even through his torpor, the words startled Gosseyn. And then he frowned in understanding: The propaganda war also was on. Everywhere he turned the dial, voices were roaring their threats and accusations. The Machine! The dastardly Machine! Mechanical monstrosity, treacherous, inhuman! The Venusian plotters who had foisted its poisonous alien will upon men. Strait jacket . . . assassin . . . massacre . . .

And all the time, as a background to the lying voices, came the thunder of the guns, the muffled, unceasing thunder of the guns. Gosseyn began to doze. Better get to bed. Tired. So tired.

"GOSSEYN!"

All the other voices blotted out. Radio talking directly to him.

"GOSSEYN, THIS IS THE MACHINE. DON'T KILL YOURSELF."

"Kill myself! I'm nobody. Everybody hates me. What's the good of being alive?"

"GOSSEYN, DON'T KILL YOURSELF. YOUR THIRD BODY HAS BEEN DESTROYED BY THE GANG. GOSSEYN, I CAN'T LAST MUCH LONGER. DURING THE FIRST HALF HOUR, NORMAL SHELLS WERE FIRED AT ME. BUT AT INTERVALS NOW ATOMIC TORPEDOES HAVE STRUCK AT MY DEFENSES.

"I HAVE A NINETY-FOOT STEEL OUTER BARRIER. GOSSEYN, IT'S BEEN PENETRATED FIVE

TIMES BY TORPEDOES THAT CAME FROM THE DIRECTION OF VENUS.

"GOSSEYN, DON'T KILL YOURSELF. YOUR THIRD BODY HAS BEEN DESTROYED. YOU MUST LEARN TO USE YOUR EXTRA BRAIN. I CAN GIVE YOU NO ADVICE ABOUT THAT BECAUSE . . ."

Crash!

There was a pause, then: "Ladies and gentlemen, the Games Machine has just been destroyed by a direct hit. Its malicious, treacherous attack on the palace has been—"

Click!

He had been intending to turn it off for some minutes. Nuisance. Telling him something about—Something —What?

Back on the bed, he lay puzzling about that. Something about—about— How tired he was! *"Kill myself. Everybody hates me. I'm ruined. What's the good of being alive? Kill myself."*

XXIII

Gosseyn's first conscious effort was to move his hands. He couldn't. He seemed to be lying on top of them. "Funny position," he thought. A vague annoyance swept him, and an awareness that he'd have to emerge further out of his hypnotic sleep to free himself.

He was about to make the effort when a memory came as to why he had come to his hotel room. Eyes closed, he waited for the will to death to surge through him. The best method, it seemed to his taut mind, was to snatch the automatic he had put on the table beside the bed and fire into his brain in one synchronized movement. But the impulse to suicide did not come. Instead, out of the depths of him welled a cheerful confidence, a buoyant sense of certain victory, a conviction that nothing could stop him. He tried to open his eyes, but couldn't. "It's the hypnotic drug," he thought in agony. "Like dope." He lay there for a moment, puzzling over his feeling in such high spirits while the drug still held him. Then came uneasy recollection—the memory of an interruption and of loud sounds. The connection was obscure, but he had seemed to get out of bed. Had he shut off the record player at that time?

"I'm sure," said a woman's voice from his left, "that you can manage now. The drug is not all-powerful."

The unexpected words did it. Gosseyn opened his eyes. Two awarenesses flashed upon him almost simultaneously. He was lying on his arms, but that wasn't the reason he couldn't use them. They were handcuffed together. And sitting in a chair beside the bed, smoking a cigarette, looking at him thoughtfully, was Patricia Hardie. Slowly, Gosseyn, who had half sat up, sank back onto his pillow. The girl took a long puff at her cigarette. Not until she had blown a lazy streamer of smoke at the ceiling did she speak. She said, "I chained you up because you're a rather dominating person with a very strong will to know things."

She laughed. It was a quiet, relaxed, wonderfully musical laugh. It startled Gosseyn. He noticed, suddenly, that she looked different. The pettish expression, that attribute of neuroticism, was gone from her. All the pleasing features of her good-looking face remained, but they were changed in a subtle fashion. Her beauty, that had been weak though bright, was revealed now in strength. Vivid as fire, her personality flamed at him. She had always been cool, sure of herself. Enhanced by her new maturity, those qualities showed magnificent. In some indefinable fashion, the pretty, headstrong girl had overnight become a glowingly alive, beautiful woman who said, "I had better get down to business. I took the risk of coming here because your action in sending the Distorter to the Games Machine has backfired. And something will have to be done about it tonight."

For Gosseyn, the pause that followed was extremely welcome. His mind was still wrapped around what she had said earlier: "You have . . . a will to know about things." He had indeed, but where did she fit into that? He was not, he realized, grasping the meaning of her presence here. Patricia Hardie had told him many things, but he had never had the impression that she herself was playing a vital part in this drama of null-A against the universe. She watched his face as he started to ask his questions. Finally she sighed. She said, "I'm not going to tell you anything. The more you know, the more dangerous you are to the rest of us. Besides, there's no time."

"Oh, there isn't!" Gosseyn spoke in exasperation. "I'm afraid that we'll just have to make time. Let me see," he continued. "There's a problem of your relationship to Hardie. Let's begin there."

The young woman sat with her eyes closed. Without opening them, she began to speak. "I'm going to be very patient with you," she said. "Im going to tell you that the Distorter is still inside the Games Machine, where you sent it. And that we must have it. It is one of the few galactic devices within our reach. We need it for evidence."

"My opinion," said Gosseyn, "of a group that is permitting two planets to be taken over without once issuing a general warning is so low that it can hardly be put into words." He stopped there. "Evidence?" he said.

She seemed not to hear the question. "You mustn't be too harsh," she said in a low voice. "We couldn't stop the attack. A warning would simply have precipitated it. And, besides, warn whom? Venus has no government. Its detective, judicial, and communications systems are controlled by the gang. The warning would have had to be general, and Eldred and I have racked our brains wondering how to do it. His only solution is that there must be a better Machine built when this is all over. It can be done, you know. At the Semantics Institute they have constructed tubes in series around highly improved lie detectors that can examine the body and mind of a man at a glance and tell the degree of null-A training he has received. That will eliminate the ponderous games. And there are other improvements that would protect the Machine against the kind of interference to which it has been subjected."

She paused, then went on: "Later, when you have rescued the Distorter, I'll tell you much more. But now, listen! There is a young man here in the hotel who will help you. He is no agent of mine, but you will find out all about him when you read this note after I leave. He, not I, was the one who saved you from the hypno. Mind you, I was here in time to have saved you from the worst effect. But he did something that I couldn't have done. Because of him, no one knows that you are in this hotel.

"And, Gilbert Gosseyn,"—she leaned forward; her eyes were a soft blue—"don't be too impatient. I admit you're being used roughly. But that's because you're out in the open. We have analyzed your position like this: You were brought out when the crisis was near. Thorson was startled, but I doubt if he intended to kill you. That was an accident. Then you reappeared in a second body, first at Prescott's hospital and then at Eldred Crang's tree house, both key points so far as the galactic empire is concerned.

"You can't imagine what a shock that was. Thorson grew immensely cautious. Discovering the untrained nature of your extra brain, he allowed himself to be persuaded to release you. That was Eldred's doing, but we didn't know that Thorson agreed to it because his agents were actually on the point of finding your third body. We still don't know where it was found. The important thing for you is that now that your third body has been destroyed, you are again a wanted man."

Gosseyn said, "Now that my third body has been what?"

For the first time since he had awakened, she looked startled.

"You mean, you don't *know?*" she breathed. "You have no idea what's been happening?" Her tone changed. "I can't stop to tell you. Read the papers." She stood up. "Remember, take the Distorter to the home of the young man downstairs. I'll meet you there some time tomorrow." She was fumbling in her purse. She drew out a key, tossed it onto the bed. "For the handcuffs," she explained. "Good-by, and good luck." The door closed behind her.

Gosseyn removed the handcuffs, and then he sat down firmly on the edge of the bed and thought, "What was she talking about?" He recalled that she had mentioned a note. His puzzled gaze, roving the room, touched the bureau to the right of the bed, behind him. A newspaper lay there, and a sheet of white paper. Gosseyn jumped for it across the bed. He read wonderingly:

Dear Mr. Gosseyn:
When I heard the news, I knew there would be a search for you. So I immediately destroyed the card showing you were registered in this hotel and substituted one for your room, 974, under the first name I could think of—John Wentworth.
Then, after I was off duty, I let myself into your room with a passkey and found you lying there with

that record going. I removed it, and recorded one of my own with the intention of counteracting all depressing effects.

I shut that off the last time I was up to look at you as I understand you can make someone light-headed by feeding him too much optimism. I hope that I struck a balance, as you'll need all your good sense in the fight ahead.

This is written by one who intended to try the games next year, who places himself completely at your service, and who dares to sign himself,

With all best wishes,

Dan Lyttle

P.S. *I'll be up again when I go off duty at midnight. Meanwhile, read the morning paper. You'll see then what I'm talking about.*

D.L.

Gosseyn reached for the paper and unfolded it on the bed. The four-inch capitals of the headline glared up at him:

GAMES MACHINE
DESTROYED

Gosseyn, trembling with excitement, read by visual leaps that took in whole paragraphs:

. . . Fired at the palace and . . . simultaneously broadcast warnings about a mysterious attack against . . . Venus (No such attack . . . taken place. See Radio Exchange report, page 3). Authorities decided . . . insane . . . following so soon on assassination of President Hardie . . . evidence linking the Machine . . . accordingly destroyed.

For an hour . . . Machine broadcast . . . incomprehensible message to Gilbert Gosseyn, whose picture is reproduced elsewhere . . . this page . . . previously exonerated . . . To be picked up again for further questioning. Arrest on sight . . .

As he read, Gosseyn remembered second by second

what the Games Machine had said over the radio. Now, swallowing hard, he looked at the photographic reproduction. it was a head view only, and it was his face all right. But there was something wrong with it. Seconds passed before he realized what it was. They had taken a photograph of the corpse of Gilbert Gosseyn I.

The amusement that came was grim. He laid the paper down and staggered over to a chair. He felt sick with reaction and with rage. He had nearly killed himself. It was so close that it was as if he had died, and this was resurrection. What did the Machine mean, ordering him to commit suicide, and then calling it off because "your third body has been destroyed!" Of all the organic matter in the world, that body of Gilbert Gosseyn III should have been protected against discovery.

His fury died slowly. Soberly he analyzed his situation. "The first move," he thought, "is to get the Distorter. Then learn how to use my extra brain."

Or was that last possible? Could he ever do that alone—he who had thought and thought about it without once producing the slightest apparent effect on that special part of his mind? He mustered an ironic smile. "I am not," he thought decisively, "going to get lost in those depths just now."

There were a number of things to do first. He disconnected the videoplate of the phone—another clerk might be on duty—and then called the desk. A pleasant voice answered. Gosseyn said, "This is John Wentworth."

There was silence at the other end, then, "Yes, sir. How are things? Dan Lyttle at this end. I'll be right up, sir."

Gosseyn waited expectantly. He remembered the clerk who had registered him as a slim, tall chap with nice features and dark hair. Lyttle in the flesh was somewhat thinner than Gosseyn's memory of him, rather weak-looking for the tough job Patricia Hardie had assigned him. He showed, however, many characteristics of null-A training, particularly in the firmness of his jaw and in the way he held himself.

"I'll have to hurry," he said.

Gosseyn frowned at that. "I'm afraid," he said, "the time has come for special risks. I have an idea an effort will be made to dismantle the destroyed Games Machine

135

as swiftly as possible. If I were confronted with such a job and wanted it done fast, I would publish a notice to the effect that anybody could have what he wanted so long as he carted it away immediately."

He saw that Dan Lyttle was staring at him wide-eyed. The young man said breathlessly, "Why, that's exactly what's been done. They're stringing up masses of lights. They say an eighth of the Machine is already gone, and that— What's the matter?"

Gosseyn was experiencing mental anguish. The Machine was gone, and hour by hour all that it stood for was going with it. Like the cathedrals and temples of far-gone days, it was a product of a creative impulse, a will to perfection which, though not dead, would never repeat itself in the same fashion. At one blow centuries of irreplaceable memories had been blotted out. It cost an effort to force the picture and the emotion out of his mind.

"There's no time to waste," he said swiftly. "If the Distorter is still inside the Machine, we have to get it. We'll have to go after it at once."

"I can't possibly leave until twelve," Lyttle protested. "We've all been ordered to remain on duty, and every hotel is being watched."

"What about your robocar—if you've got one?"

"It's parked on the roof, but I beg you not to"—his tone was earnest—"not to go up there and try to get it. I'm sure you'd be arrested immediately."

Gosseyn hesitated. He recognized consciously that he was not easily turned aside these days. At last, reluctantly, he nodded acceptance of defeat.

"You'd better get back to work," he said quietly. "We've got five hours to pass."

As silently as he had come, Lyttle slipped out and was gone.

XXIV

Left to his own resources, Gosseyn ordered food sent up to his room. By the time it arrived, he was planning his evening. He looked up a telephone number. "I want a visual connection," he said into the mouthpiece, "with the nearest phonolibrary. The number is—"

To the robot in charge at the library he explained his general wants. Within a minute, a picture was forming on the reconnected videoplate. Gosseyn sat then, eating and looking and listening. He knew what he wanted—a suggestion as to how he should begin training his extra brain. Whether or not the subject matter selected by the librarian had any relevancy to that desire was not clear. He forced himself to be patient. When the voice began with an account of the positive and negative neural excitations experienced by the simple life forms of the sea, Gosseyn settled down determinedly. He had an evening to pass.

Phrases came to him, clung as he turned them over in his mind, and then faded out of his consciousness as he discarded them. As the voice traced the growth of the nervous system on Earth, the pictures on the video changed, showing ever more complex neural interconnections until finally the comparatively high forms of life were reached, complex creatures that could learn lessons from experience. A worm bumped two hundred times against an electric current before it finally turned aside, and then, when put to the test again, turned aside after sixty shocks. A pike separated from a minnow by an almost invisible screen nearly killed itself trying to get through, and when it was finally convinced that it couldn't, not even the removal of the screen made any difference; it continued to ignore the minnow as something unobtainable. A pig went insane when confronted with a complicated path to its food.

All the experiments were shown. First the worm, then the pike actually threshing against the screen, the pig squealing madly, and, later on, a cat, a dog, a coyote, and a monkey put through their experiments. And still there was nothing that Gosseyn could use—no suggestion, no comparison that seemed to have anything to do with what he wanted.

"Now," said the voice, "before we turn to the human brain, it is worth while to note that in all these animals one limitation has again and again and again revealed itself. Without exception they identify their surroundings on a too narrow basis. The pike, after the screen was removed, continued to identify its environment on the basis of the pain it had experienced when the screen was in place. The coyote failed to distinguish between the man with the gun and the man with the camera.

"In each case, a similarity that did not exist was assumed. The story of the dark ages of the human mind is the story of man's dim comprehension that he was more than an animal, but it is a story told against a background of mass animal actions, rooted in a pattern of narrow animal identifications. The story of null-A, on the other hand, is the story of man's fight to train his brain to distinguish between similar yet different object-events in space-time. Curiously, the scientific experiments of this enlightened period show a progressive tendency to attain refinements of similarity in method, in timing, and in the structure of the materials used. It might indeed be said that science is striving to force similarity because only thus—"

Gosseyn had been listening impatiently, waiting for the discussion on the human brain to being. Now, abruptly, he thought, "What was that? *What was that?*"

He had to hold himself in his chair, to relax, to remember. And then, and not till then, did he climb to his feet and pace the floor in the burning excitement of an immeasurably great discovery made. To force a greater approximation of similarity. What else could it be? And the method of forcing would have to be through memory.

Perfect memory was, literally, a replay in the mind of an event exactly as it had originally been recorded. The brain, obviously, could only repeat its own perceptions. What it failed to retain of the process level in Nature, it would—naturally—fail to similarize. The abstraction principle of General Semantics applied. Abstraction of perceptions.

So that, basically, what was involved was a greater awareness of that which made up a person's identity: the memory stored in the brain and elsewhere in the body. The more he strove for perfect memory, the more clearly demarcated an individual he would be.

. . . *What else could it be*? There just wasn't any other possibility that offered as logical a continuity of the developing of the null-A idea. But what good would it be when he finally achieved it?

He grew aware that somewhere a clock was striking. Gosseyn glanced at his watch, and sighed with excitement at the realization that the time for action had come.

Midnight.

XXV

Masses of parked cars, moving figures, shafts of near light, a distant blaze, confusion. After they parked their car about a mile from the central glare, Gosseyn and Lyttle followed a thin stream of people for half a mile. They came at last to where other people were standing, watching. That was where the really hard part began. Even for a null-A it was difficult to think of a third-of-a-mile barrier of human beings as if each unit was an individual with a personality and a will of its own.

The mob swayed or stood still. It had volitions that began like a tiny snowball rolling downhill and setting off an avalanche. There were gasps as people were crushed by the pressures; there were shrieks as the unlucky lost their foothold and went down. The crowd was a soulless woman; it reared up on its toes and stared mindlessly at those who were feasting on the destroyed symbol of a world's sanity.

Swarms of roboplanes whirred overhead, weighted with loot. But that wasn't so bad. If only that method of transport had been used, the danger would have been minimized. Trucks were also being used—lines of trucks with glaring lights, driven at top speed, straight at the fringes of crowd that constantly threatened to overlap the roads. Shaken and frightened, the mob kept its skirts drawn back.

Slowly, Gosseyn and Lyttle worked their way along the dangerous path to the Machine. They had to keep their eyes open for rifts in the packs of trucks; they had to strain to see pockets in the masses of human beings, pockets toward which they could run in the desperate hope that the space would not be filled up when they got there. In spite of the risk, it did not surprise Gosseyn that they made progress. There was a curious psychological law that protected men with purposes from those who had none.

The important thing was not to arouse counterpurpose. Once, when they were penned in by an apparently endless line of racing trucks, Gosseyn shouted, "This is the city side! The mountain slopes on the other side probably have hardly anyone on them. When we leave, we'll go that way and work around to your car."

They came to a steel fence that enterprising wrecking crews had put up against the crowd. It was for the most part a successful barrier, and the occasional individual who vaulted over it usually slunk back before the threatening guns of the guards who stood in little groups on the other side of the fence, like soldiers lawfully guarding a property from vandals.

Once more, it was a case of straightforward risk. "Keep close to the road!" Gosseyn yelled. "They'll hesitate about shooting at the trucks."

The moment they broke into the open, two guards raced toward them, shrieking something that was lost in the bedlam. Their contorted faces were limned in the fitful light. Their guns waved ferociously. And they went down like briefly animated dummies as Gosseyn shot them. He ran on after Lyttle, startled. He who had so frequently refused to kill—merciless now. The guards were symbols, he decided bleakly, symbols of destruction. Having taken on unhuman qualities, they were barbarous entities, to be destroyed like attacking beasts and forgotten. He forgot them. Ahead was the remnant of the Games Machine.

For hours Gosseyn had tied his hopes to a law of logic. A law which held that a machine which had taken years to build couldn't be unbuilt in twenty-four hours. He was not so right as he had expected. The Machine was visibly smaller. But it was the torpedo damage that was responsible. The outer tiers of game rooms were caved-in husks, as if fantastic air pressures had smashed them. And everywhere thirty-, fifty-, ninety-foot holes gaped in the gleaming, dented walls. Black, jagged holes that revealed, under the spraying, glittering light, torn masses of scintillating wires and instruments—the outer portions of the nervous system of the dead Machine.

For the first time, standing there, Gosseyn thought of the Machine as a high-type organism that had been living and was now dead. What was intelligent life but the sen-

140

tive awareness of a nervous sytem with a memory of experiences? In all the man-known history of the world, here never had been an organism with so much memory, uch a vast experience, such a tremendous knowledge of uman beings and human nature, as the Games Machine. 'ar in the background of his mind Gosseyn heard Dan Lyttle cry, "Come along! We mustn't delay."

Gosseyn recognized that was so and moved forward, but t was his body that followed Lyttle toward the realization f their purpose. His mind and gaze clung to the Machine. Seen at closer range, the extent of the salvage work was more apparent. Whole sections had been torn down, were being torn down, were about to be torn down. Men carrying machines and metal plates and instruments swarmed out of the dark passageways; the sight of them shocked Gosseyn. Once more he was stopped by the realization that he was witnessing the end of an era.

Lyttle tugged at his arm. And that galvanized Gosseyn as no words could have. He hurried forward, skirting the fiery glare of the truck and plane lights, the blaze of the beacons that poured down from every projection of metal big enough to support an atomic-powered searchlight.

"Around to the back," Gosseyn called, and led the way to the overhanging fold of metal into which the truck had disappeared with the crate containing the Distorter. As they half ran the din retreated somewhat, and there were not so many planes or trucks or men.

There was tremendous activity, of course. The hissing of cutters, the clang of metal falling, the confusion of movement—all were there, but in lesser quantity. For every hundred men and trucks in the front of the Machine, there were a score here, working just as hard, just as frantically, apparently conscious that it was only a matter of time until their easy possession was challenged by irresistible numbers. And still the din grew less. Gosseyn and Lyttle came to the flange behind which the Distorter had been taken, and saw a scant dozen trucks drawn up against a loading platform. Doors had been cut out of the front of an enormous shedlike room, and from this vast, dim area men were carrying packing cases, machines, pieces of metal, and instruments.

The shed was almost empty, and the crate with the

Distorter in it stood off by itself as if waiting for them
An address had been stamped on it in six-inch black letters:

RESEARCH DEPARTMENT
THE SEMANTIC INSTITUTE
KORZYBSKI SQUARE
CITY

The address started a chain of thought in Gosseyn's
mind. The Machine was under the legal control of the
Institute. Since it knew a lot, then perhaps the people there
knew more. It was a point to investigate as soon as possible.

They headed out into the open field, out into the
darkness. The sounds died behind them. The glare of light
retreated beyond the peak of a high hill. They reached the
car and arrived presently in the yard of the neat little home
of Dan Lyttle. In a vague fashion Gosseyn had believed
that Patricia Hardie would be waiting there for him. But
she wasn't.

There was an excitement about removing the Distorter
from its crate that took away the empty feeling of her not
being there. They laid the Distorter, face upward, on the
floor, and then sat down and looked at it. Bright, steely
alien metal—world destroyer! Because of it the agents of a
galactic conqueror had reached into all the high places of
Earth, and for long, oh, far too long, it was unsuspected.
His initial capture of the Distorter had proved to be one of
the final steps in the crisis of null-A.

Finding itself free, the Games Machine had broadcast
the truth and brought the Venusian war to Earth. For better or worse, the forces of the invaders and of null-A were
now engaged, or about to be engaged. Sitting there, Gosseyn felt a black dismay. From every logical angle, the
fight was already lost. He saw that Lyttle was tired. The
young man's head drooped. He caught Gosseyn's eyes on
him and he smiled grayly.

"I was in such a state of tension yesterday," he said,
"that I didn't sleep a wink. I intended to buy some anti-
sleep pills, but I forgot."

Gosseyn said, "Lie down on the couch and sleep if you can."

"And miss what you're going to do? Not on your life."

Gosseyn smiled at that. He explained that he intended to conduct his examination of the Distorter on an orderly basis.

"First of all, I want to locate the source of energy used by the tubes, and so be able to switch it on or off. I'll need some simple equipment, and the investigation itself will take time. Show me where you keep the instruments you used for taking your course in null-A physics and then go to sleep."

In three minutes, he was on his own. He felt in no hurry. From the beginning he had moved along at dizzying speeds and got approximately nowhere. The world of null-A, which he had once thought he was supposed to save, was crashing, *had* crashed, around him.

But just what did he expect out of this examination? A clue, Gosseyn decided. Some key to its operation. Patricia had said it was forbidden—presumably by that weak organization the Galactic League, yet she had mentioned that its use was permitted for transport. What had that meant? He picked up Lyttle's energy scanner and began adjusting the meter on it, peering from time to time through the eyehole. Abruptly, he could see into the Distorter.

What made the first observation simple was that he could not see into the tubes. Their intricacies withheld, the problem of organizing the complication inside the Distorter became a matter of following the wire system. Gosseyn searched for the power source. He didn't have to go far because *the power was on.* He had taken it for granted that the Machine would have shut the thing off. It took ten minutes to convince him that there was no apparent way of switching off the power. It was on. And meant to stay on. The Games Machine, of course, would have used energy probers that could short-circuit a wire system right through metal, and so it had solved its special problems. Gilbert Gosseyn, lacking a prober, was stymied, and since he had virtually promised Lyttle that he would do nothing on his own, he decided to go to sleep. It was possible that by the time he awakened Patricia would have arrived.

But she hadn't. There was no one around. It was half past four in the afternoon and, except for the Distorter, he was alone in the house. There was a note from Lyttle on the kitchen table to the effect that he had gone to work and that he was leaving the car for Gosseyn to use. The note finished:

> . . . what the radio calls "murderous elements" are beginning to sabotage "peaceful production" and they are to be "ruthlessly" put down by the forces of "law and order."
> You'll find food all around you. I'll be back at 12:30.
> Dan Lyttle

After he had eaten, Gosseyn went into the living room and stared down at the Distorter, dissatisfied with his whole position. "I'm here," he thought, "in a house where I could be captured in five minutes. There are at least two persons in the city who know I am in this house."

It wasn't that he didn't trust Patricia and Lyttle. He had made the assumption out of things that had happened, out of actual events, that they were on his side. But it was disquieting to be dependent again in any way upon the actions of other people. It wasn't distrust. But suppose something had gone wrong. Suppose at this very minute information was being pressed out of Patricia about where he was, about the Distorter.

He couldn't go out until dark. Which left the Distorter. Undecided, he knelt beside it, and, reaching out gingerly, he touched the corner tube nearest him. Just what he expected he wasn't sure. But he was prepared for shock. The tube was vaguely warm against his fingers. Gosseyn caressed it for a moment, rueful, irritated at his caution. "If I decide to leave in a hurry," he thought, "I'll grab a handful of tubes and take them along with me."

He stood up. "I'll give her till dark." He hesitated, frowning again. Maybe he'd better get those tubes now. They might not come out easily.

He was sitting examining the Distorter again through the scanner when the phone rang. It was Lyttle, his voice shaking with excitement.

"I'm calling from a pay phone. I've just seen the latest paper. It says that Patricia Hardie was arrested an hour and a half ago for—get this, it's monstrous—the murder of her father. Mr. Wentworth"—Lyttle's question was strangely timid—"how long does it take to make a null-A talk?"

"There is no set time," said Gosseyn. He was cold, his mind like a steel bar that had been struck a mighty blow and was now vibrating strongly in response. Thorson was playing this game implacably. He found his voice again.

"Listen," he said. "I'll have to let you decide for yourself whether or not you stick to your job until midnight. If you know somewhere that you can go, go at once. If you feel that you have to come back here, come with care. I might or might not leave the Distorter here. I'm going to remove some tubes from it and go—well, never mind. Watch the 'Careless'-'Guest' ads in the paper. And thanks for everything, Dan."

He waited, but when there was no comment, he hung up. Straight for the Distorter he headed. The corner tube, like all the others, projected about an inch above the metal. He grasped it and pulled at it with a slowly increasing pressure. It wouldn't come out.

He reversed his effort and pushed instead of pulled. There was probably a catch that needed releasing. The tube clicked down. There was a sudden, sharp strain on his eyes. The room wavered—his amazement was conscious, and the answer, the realization of what was happening was equally clear—wavered, vibrated, trembled in every molecule. Shook like an image in a crystal-clear pool into which a stone has been violently tossed.

His head began to ache. He fumbled with his fingers, searching for the tube, but it was hard to see. He closed his eyes briefly, but it made no difference. The tube was burning hot under the fingers with which he tried to pull it back into place. He must have been dazed because he swayed and fell forward, bumping against the Distorter. He had a strange sense of lightness.

He opened his eyes in surprise. He was lying on his side in utter darkness, and in his nostrils was the rich odor of growing wood. It was a familiar, heavy scent, but it took Gosseyn a long moment to make the enormous mental jump necessary to grasping the reality of it. The odor was the same as had assailed him on his futile journey into the tree tunnel behind Crang's house on Venus.

Gosseyn scrambled to his feet, almost fell as he stumbled over something metallic, and then groped against first one upcurving wall, then the other. And there was no doubt. He was in a tunnel in the roots of a gigantic tree of Venus.

XXVI

Nevertheless, the consuming hunger of the uncritical mind for what it imagines to be certainty or finality impels it to feast upon shadows

E.T.B.

The burst of energy that had galvanized him into verifying where he was subsided. Gosseyn sat down heavily. It was not altogether a voluntary action. His hands were shaking; his knees felt weak.

He had already noticed it was dark. Now he realized it with a new intensity. Darkness! Shadowless, unrelenting darkness. It pressed against his eyes and into his brain. He could feel his clothes against his skin, and the pressure of the wood floor. But in this night they could have been vagrant titillations experienced by a bodiless entity. In this unrelieved blackness, substance, human or unhuman, was almost a meaningless term.

"I can," Gosseyn told himself, "last two weeks without food, three days without water."

He recognized that he didn't feel as hopeless as that, in spite of his memory of miles of black tunnels. Because they wouldn't have focused a Distorter tube on just any part of this Venusian tree tunnel. It must be near some special point, easily accessible from where he was.

He was about to climb to his feet when he realized for the first time the magnitude of what had happened. A few minutes ago he had been on Earth. Now he was on Venus.

What was it Prescott had said? "If two energies can be attuned on a twenty-decimal approximation of similarity, the greater will bridge the gap of space between them just

146

as if there were no gap, although the juncture is accomplished at finite speeds."

The finite speeds involved had been infinite for all the practical purposes of solar distances. Gosseyn began to feel better. The Distorter had attuned the highly organized energy compound that was his body to this small section of tree tunnel, and the "greater" had bridged the gap of space to the "lesser."

Gosseyn stood up and thought, "Why, I'm on Venus—where I wanted to be." His spirits lifted higher. In spite of all his mistakes, he was still safe, still progressing. He knew many things, and even what he did not know suddenly seemed attainable. He had but to see more deeply, make a few more abstractions from reality, refine his observations another decimal place, and the veil would be torn aside, the mystery comprehended by his senses.

The thought in its implications was wide enough in scope to actuate the integration "pause" of his nervous system. He grew even calmer.

He remembered the metal on which he had stumbled when he had first tried to get to his feet. Even in that darkness, he found the object within seconds. It was the Distorter, as he had half anticipated. Cautiously his fingers touched each of the four corner tubes in turn. It was the fourth tube that was depressed, *still* depressed. Gosseyn hesitated. The Distorter had been "set" by people who had their own purposes and destinations. Some of the tubes were designed to "interfere" with the Games Machine, but a few surely could transport him to other parts of the solar system, possibly to key centers of gang activity—military headquarters, the secret galactic base, storehouses of atomic torpedoes.

The potentialities startled him. But they weren't for now. This was not the time to take risks or conduct experiments. The sooner he got away from here the better.

Gingerly, he picked up the Distorter and began to walk along in the darkness.

"I'll walk a thousand steps in one direction," he decided, "then come back and walk a thousand in the other direction." That should bring him to the gang center near his point of "landing." They wouldn't have put it further away that that.

As he rounded a sharp bend in the tunnel, after approximately three hundred steps, he saw a glimmer of light. He rounded three more bends. Even then the glow, though bright now and dead ahead, was sourceless. But Gosseyn saw that there was a railing silhouetted against the light. He put down the Distorter.

Cautiously he moved forward. At the last moment, he dropped to his hands and knees. An instant later, he was staring between the bars of the fence. There was a metal pit below him. The metal gleamed dully from scores of atomic lights that blazed at set intervals from the enormous, downcurving walls. The pit was about two miles long, a mile wide, and half a mile deep. And, occupying one half of the far end, was a ship. It was a ship such as Earth men might have dreamed about in their wilder imaginative soarings. Spaceship engineers, plan-happy after weeks of poring over ninety-foot draft plans of normal solar spaceships, might have gone home and babbled to their wives, "Now I'm going to take off five hundred years and start a million draftsmen drawing plans for an interstellar ship two miles long."

The ship in the pit was just under two miles long. Its ridged back reared up sharklike to within what seemed a hundred feet of the ceiling. Another ship of its own size could have lain beside it, but if it had, the two of them would have crowded the mile width of the pit.

Distance obscured details, but even so Gosseyn could see tiny figures swarming on the metal under the great belly of the ship. They seemed to have contact with something below the floor, for every little while great batches of little shapes scurried from a long line of humps that projected from the floor—as if elevators had come up loaded from floors lower down and disgorged their cargo. In the diagonal way Gosseyn was looking down at them, they must have been at least two-thirds of a mile away, little dark things crawling over the metal.

Gosseyn saw with a start that the ship was getting ready to leave. The minute figures below were clambering up steps into it. There were a hundred dark moving shapes—a dozen—none. A vague throb of sound had come from them, movements, a whisper of conversation. Now silence settled over the blazing vastness of the pit. Gosseyn waited.

It would be complete night outside. They'd need night for the movement of such ships. In a moment the ceiling would start opening. There'd be a meadow above, camouflage for the hangars below. It would be pushed up somehow.

As he watched, all the lights went out. That, also, fitted. They wouldn't want a light shining up into the night. Sensitive detectors must be probing the skies, to make sure no roboplanes or other solar craft were passing overhead. But it was the ship that took on life, not the ceiling.

The ship began to glow. A weak, all-over radiance it was that outlined every square foot of its body; a vaguely green light, so dim that Earth's moonlight would have been sun-bright beside it. It began to shimmer. Abruptly, it hurt his eyes.

Gosseyn recalled that the Distorter had affected him the same way. He thought, "The ship! It's being attuned to a planetary base of some other star. There isn't any ceiling opening." As swiftly as it had started, the mental and visual strain ended. The green haze jerked and winked out.

The great ship was gone.

Below, in the pit, four of the lights came back on. They were as bright as miniature suns, but their white fire was only a partial match for the normal darkness of the pit. Near them, everything was brilliantly illuminated. But the glare dimmed as the glow spread out through the cubic vastness of the hangar. Hundreds of acres in the center and between the wall lights were deep in shadow.

Gosseyn picked up the Distorter and began to follow the railing around the pit's edge. He wasn't sure what he was looking for. Certainly he had no desire to go down into the pit. Somewhere along here must be a way out of these tree roots. A stairway, an elevator, *something*.

It turned out to be an elevator. Rather a row of elevator shafts with elevators in two of the shafts. Gosseyn tried the door catch of the first one. It slid open without a sound. He stepped in boldly and examined the control apparatus. It was more complicated than he had expected. There was bank of tubes, but no control lever. Gosseyn

149

felt the blood drain from his face as he realized what it was. A Distorter-type elevator. It wouldn't only go up and down. It would go to any one of—he counted the tubes—twelve destinations.

He groaned inwardly and bent to examine each tube carefully for markings. It was then he saw, with relief, that each tube was shaped to point in a different direction. Only one of them pointed straight up. Gosseyn did not hesitate. It might take him into instant captivity, but that was a danger he had to risk. His fingers touched the tube and pressed down.

This time he tried to watch the sensation. But the anesthesia that blurred his senses affected his brain. When his vision cleared, he saw that the scene outside the elevator had changed.

He was very definitely in a tree. Beyond the transparent door of the elevator was an unpolished, natural "room." Light splashed down on it from a hole higher up. It was all very rough and uneven, and there were many dark corners.

It was in one of the dark corners that Gosseyn hid the Distorter, and then cautiously he climbed up toward the hole. The corridor mounted steeply ahead of him, narrowing steadily. Halfway up, he realized he wouldn't be able to get the Distorter through. That was jarring, but he decided he couldn't let it make any difference. He had to contact the Venusians. Later, with their help, he could come back for the Distorter.

During the final third of the climb, he had to use his hands and clutch at projecting edges of dry-rotted wood to pull himself up. He came out on a lower limb of a titanic Venusian tree, through a hole that was only about twice as big as his body. It was an unevenly shaped, natural-looking hole. It was probably one of hundreds of similar holes in this very tree, and therefore he would have to mark its location very carefully.

He had already noticed that there was a great meadow on one side of him—over the pit, perhaps. In the opposite direction was dense Venusian forest. Gosseyn picked out landmarks, and then started along the broad limb onto which he had emerged. About seventy-five yards from the bole it joined an equally massive limb of another tree. He felt a thrill as he saw it. There was a thalamic pleasure in tree running. The Venusians must indulge in it often for the sheer animal joy of it. He would remain aloft for about five miles, unless the forest ended first, and then——

He had proceeded about fifty feet along the limb when the bark under him collapsed. He fell down onto a floor. Instantly, the long trapdoor above him closed, and he was in darkness. Gosseyn scarcely noticed the absence of light. Because, as he hit the smooth floor, *it* tilted downward. Tilted sharply, fifty, sixty, seventy degrees. Gosseyn made one desperate leap upward. His fingers clawed against smooth wood, then slid off into emptiness. He hit the floor again, hard, and slid down that steep incline. It was not a long journey that he took then, not more than thirty feet. But its implications were bottomless. He was caught.

He had no intention of giving up. Even while he was still sliding, Gosseyn fought to get to his feet, fought to turn, to *return* before the floor could rise back into place out of his reach. He failed. In the very act of whirling, of flinging himself, he heard the click of the floor fitting itself into position above him. And still he did not pause. He jumped to the uttermost height that his strength would take him, and reached into the darkness with clawing fingers that groped only at air. This time he gathered himself for the fall and landed on his feet, balanced, conscious that if there was a way of escape he must find it within minutes. And yet, for a moment, he forced himself to stand still, to make the null-A cortical-thalamic pause, to think.

So far everything had seemed automatic. The section of tree limb had caved in because he had put his weight upon it. The floor had tilted for the same reason. The fact that such trapdoors existed was depressing. Alarms would be ringing. He'd have to find a way out before anybody came, or never!

He dropped to his knees, made a swinging but relaxed sweep of the floor. To his right, he touched a rug. He crawled over the rug and in seconds had fingered a chest of drawers, a table, an easy chair, and a bed. A bedroom! There'd be a light switch, perhaps a table lamp or bed light. His swift thought paused there, yielded to action.

The wall switch clicked under his fingers, and so, approximately three minutes after his first fall, he was able to see his prison.

It was not bad. There were twin beds, but they were in a large alcove of coral pink that opened onto a large living room at least as big, at least as luxurious, as the one in Crang's apartment. The furniture had the glowing quality of fine wood beautifully finished. There were paintings on the walls, but Gosseyn did not pause to look at them because his restless gaze had lighted on a closed door. A sound came from it, a key clicking in the lock.

Gosseyn drew back, drawing his guns. As the door opened, he saw a robogun floating there. And the voice of Jim Thorson called out, "All right, Gosseyn, drop your weapons and submit to a search."

There was nothing else to do. A moment later, after soldiers had come in and relieved him of his weapons, the gun drew back. And Jim Thorson came through the door.

XXVII

On a cliff of metal on the planet of beasts, the League ambassador landed. He walked slowly over to the parapet of that vast building and stared uneasily down at the jungle four miles below.

"I suppose," he thought, "I'll be expected to go hunting with the"——he paused, searched for the right word, then grimly——"extroverts who build hunting lodges as big as this."

A voice behind him murmured, "This way, Your Excellency. The hunting party will leave in an hour, and Enro the Red will confer with you en route."

"Tell His Excellency, the foreign minister of the Greatest Empire," the ambassador began firmly, "that I have just arrived, and that——"

He stopped, the refusal unspoken. No one, least of all League agents, turned down the invitations of the reigning overlord of an empire of sixty thousand star systems, especially when one's purpose required considerable tact. The ambassador finished quietly, "—and that I will be ready in time."

It was a bloodthirsty business. There were guns for each type of beast, carried by noiseless machines, one machine for each hunter. The robots were always at hand, holding out just the right weapon, yet they never got in the way. The most dangerous animals were held off by energy screens while the hunters maneuvered for firing position.

There was one long, sleek, powerful, hoofed animal, gray in color, which realized after one burst of effort that it was trapped. It sat down on its haunches and began to cry. Enro the Red himself put a bullet through its nearest eye. It pitched over and lay sobbing and writhing for a minute, then grew still. Afterward, on the way back to that gigantic combination hunting lodge and alternate foreign office, the red-haired giant came over to the League ambassador.

"Great sport, eh?" he growled. "Though I notice you didn't shoot much."

"This is my first time," apologized the other. "I was fascinated."

That was true enough, if you thought of it in a certain way. Fascinated, horrified, shocked, disgusted. He saw that the great man was staring at him sardonically.

"You League men are all the same," Enro said. "A bunch of cowardl—" He stopped. He seemed to think better of his harsh indictment. "Peaceable!" he said.

"You must remember," the ambassador said coolly, "that the League was organized by the nineteen galactic empires at a time when they were destroying each other in futile and indecisive wars. Peace is the trade of the League, and, like all institutions, it has gradually created men who actually *think* peace."

"Sometimes," said Enro proudly, "I believe I prefer war, however destructive."

The League officer said nothing, and presently Enro ceased chewing on his lower lip and said curtly, "Well, what is it you wish?"

The ambassador began diplomatically, "We have recently discovered that your transportation ministry has been overzealous."

"In what way?"

"The case to which I refer is that of a sun system called Sol by its dominant inhabitants."

"The name does not strike a memory chord," Enro said coldly.

The ambassador bowed. "It will undoubtedly be on record in your department, and the problem is very simple. A transit base was established there by your transport department about five hundred years ago without permission from the League. Sol is one of the systems discovered after the agreements were signed respecting the exploration and exploitation of new-found stars."

"Hm-m!" The red one's gaze was even more sardonic, and the ambassador thought, Enro *did* know about Sol! Enro said, "And are you going to give us permission to keep the base there?"

"It must be dismantled and removed," the League man said firmly, "as prescribed by the articles of the League charter."

"It seems a very minor affair," said Enro thoughtfully. "Leave a memorandum with my transport secretary and I will have it looked into."

"But the base will be dismantled?" said the ambassador determinedly.

Enro was cool. "Not necessarily. After all, if it's been there a long time, it might cause considerable dislocation to the transport department to have it removed. If that is so, we will take the matter up with the League and seek confirmation of our position there. Such incidents are bound to happen in vast stellar organizations. They must be handled in a progressive and elastic fashion."

It was the smaller man's turn to be sardonic. "I'm sure Your Excellency would be the first to protest if some other empire accidentally added a star system to its possessions. The League attitude is very clear. Those who made the mistake must rectify it."

Enro was scowling. "We will take the matter up at the next League session."

"But that is a year away."

Enro seemed not to hear. "I seem to remember something about this system now. Very bloodthirsty inhabitants, if my memory serves me correctly. Disorder or war

154

f some kind going on there right now."

He smiled grimly. "We shall ask permission to reestablish order. I am sure that the League delegates will ot object to that."

XXVIII

omberly, Gosseyn watched as his enemy strode into the edroom. It would be Thorson rather than Crang. Even rescott would have been preferable. But Thorson it was—looming giant of a man with gray-green eyes, strong, eavy face, and dominating hawk nose. His lips twisted he faintest bit. His nostrils dilated and contracted oticeably as he breathed. His head bent slightly to the ight as he motioned Gosseyn to a chair. He did not sit lown himself. He said with a show of concern, "Did the all hurt?"

Gosseyn dismissed the question with a shrug. "No."

"Good."

There was silence. Gosseyn had time to collect himself. His bitterness over his recapture began to fade. It couldn't be helped. A man in an enemy stronghold was at a disadvantage and continuously in danger. Even if he had known for certain that there were ambushes, he could only have gone forward as he had done.

He braced to the situation. He thought back over his relationship with Thorson, and it was not as violent as it might have been. The man had yielded several times in his favor. He had refrained from murdering him out of hand. He had even been persuaded to free him. *That* would probably not happen again, but the danger from Thorson would never be fixed and unchanging so long as he had tongue to speak. He waited.

Thorson stroked his chin. "Gosseyn," he said, "the attack on Venus has reached a curious stage. If conditions were normal, it might even be said to have failed. . . . Ah, I thought that would interest you. But whether the failure stands or not depends entirely on how receptive you are to an idea I have in mind."

"Failed!" echoed Gosseyn. At that point he had stopped listening. He thought, "I couldn't have heard him correctly." Slowly, then, the meaning pressed upon him, and still he could not bring himself to believe. A hundred times he had tried to picture the invasion of Venus: The planet of colossal trees and perpetually marvelous climate attacked everywhere at once! Men dropping from the skies in such numbers that all the hazy heavens over cities he himself had never seen would be darkened by their falling shapes! Unarmed millions surprised by trained soldiers equipped with every conceivable type of weapon in unlimited quantities! It seemed incredible that such an assault had already failed.

Thorson said slowly, "No one but myself realizes the failure as yet, except possibly"—he hesitated—"Crang." He stood frowning for a moment as at a secret thought. "Gosseyn, if you had been planning the defense on Venus, what precautions would you have taken against an attacking force that could theoretically muster more major weapons than you had men?".

Gosseyn hesitated. He had had a few thoughts about the defense of Venus, but he had no intention of telling Thorson. "I haven't the faintest idea," he said.

"What would you have done if you had been caught in the assault?"

"Why, I'd have headed for the nearest forest."

"Suppose you were married? What would you have done with your wife and children?"

"They'd have come with me, of course." He was beginning to glimpse the truth, and the vision was dazzling.

Thorson cursed. He smashed his right fist into his left palm. "But what would be the idea of that?" He said angrily. "Nobody takes women and children into the open. Our men had orders to treat the populace with consideration and respect, except where there was resistance."

Gosseyn nodded, but couldn't speak for a moment. There were tears in his eyes, tears of excitement and also of the first realization of the heavy losses that must already have been sustained. He said uneasily, "Their problem would have been to get hold of guns. How did they do that?"

Thorson groaned, and paced the floor. "It's fantastic," he said. He shrugged, walked over to a wall instrument, touched a dial, and then stepped back. "You might as well

156

get that picture straightened out before we go any further."

As he finished, the room darkened. A square patch of light brightened the wall. The light changed, deepened; the picture that formed took on a developing reality. To Gosseyn came the impression they were looking out of a window onto a noisy, troubled day scene. The window, and they with it, moved forward, turned, and showed towering trees to one side and on the level ground below men sleeping. Men by the thousands. They wore green uniforms of very light material. They looked strange, so many of them sleeping in the light of day. They kept stirring, tossing in their sleep, and there was never a moment when scores of them were not sitting up, rubbing their eyes, and then sinking back again to sleep some more.

Sentries walked along the rows and rows of sleeping men. Machines floated in the air above them, turning, twisting, their guns pointing now this way, now that, as if they, like the men, were also uneasy.

Two of the sentries walked beneath the "window" through which Gosseyn and Thorson gazed. One spoke to the other in a language Gosseyn had never heard before. He had already guessed that these were galactic soldiers, but the sound of their alien tongue jarred him, chilled him. Thorson's voice came from near his shoulder, softly:

"They're Altairans. We didn't bother to give them the local language."

Local language! Gosseyn took that in silence. The pictures that formed in his mind whenever he thought of a galactic empire and its myriad peoples were on a nonverbal level.

He was just beginning to wonder why Thorson was showing him the curious scene when he saw a movement on one, then the others, of the mighty trees. Tiny human figures—they seemed tiny against that background—were scrambling down the caves and tunnels, the enormous corrugations and indentations of the bark. As Gosseyn watched tensely, they reached the ground and raced forward, shouting. It was a strange sight, for they dropped down like monkeys from the thick lower branches, and they carried short clubs. At first they made a thin trickle, then there was a small stream, then a river, then a flood, and then they were everywhere, men in light brown shorts and brown sandals, carrying clubs. The forest swarmed like an anthill, but these ants had the shapes of men and they yelled like madmen.

The machines woke up first. Long lines of floating blasters sent their sizzling fire at the attackers. Automatically aimed weapons added their thunder to the bedlam. There were shrieks, and men went down by the hundreds. And now the camp was waking up. Cursing soldiers leaped to their feet and clutched hand weapons. Men with swinging clubs grappled them, and as the minutes lengthened there were more and more men with clubs. Above the melee of battle, the automatic weapons stuttered uncertainly, as if they were no longer sure of just where they should fire. As the sizzling of the blasters and the thunder of the weapons lessened, the sound of men cursing and grunting and breathing came clearer.

It was the awkwardness of the fighting, the close-in awkwardness of it, that suddenly enlightened Gosseyn.

"My God," he said, "is that fight going on in darkness?"

The question was rhetorical, for he could see now the difference between daylight and the daylight out there. This was a scene of the night taken by radaric cameras. From behind him, Thorson said thickly, "That's where all weapons fail. Darkness. Every man has a device for seeing in the night, but it takes power to operate it, and you have to fit it into place." He moaned with anger. "It's enough to drive you mad, to watch those stupid fools acting like all the stupid soldiers that ever were."

He raved on for another minute, then stopped. There was silence behind Gosseyn, and then Thorson spoke in a much calmer voice.

"What am I getting heated up about?" he said. "That attack took place the first night. It happened in every camp established by our soldiers. It was devastating, because no one expected unarmed hordes to attack one of the best equipped armies in the galaxy."

Gosseyn scarcely heard. He watched the battle with utter fascination. The attackers now numbered thousands. Their dead lay sometimes three deep stretching from every tree. But they were not alone. Here and there in that overwhelmed camp galactic soldiers were still struggling.

Hand blasters still flashed with an occasional murderous thrust, but as often as not, now, the wielder was a Venusian null-A.

In ten minutes more, there was no doubt of the result. And army of determined men with clubs had seized a modern military camp with all its equipment.

XXIX

As the victorious Venusians began to dig graves for the dead, Thorson reached over and switched off the video. The light in the apartment brightened. He glanced matter of factly at his watch.

"I've got less than an hour before Crang comes," he said.

He stood for a moment, frowning, then motioned at the blank wall where the video scene had been so vividly pictured a moment before.

"Naturally," he said, "we rushed in reinforcements and they made no attempt to attack cities. But that wasn't their purpose. They wanted weapons, and they got them. This is the fourth day of the invasion. As of this morning, more than twelve hundred of our spaceships have been captured and another thousand destroyed, countless weapons have been seized and turned against us, and some two million of our men killed. To accomplish that the Venusians have lost ten million people—five million killed and another five millon injured. But in my judgment their worst losses are over, whereas"—gloomily—"ours are just beginning."

He paused in the center of the room. His eyes were sullen. He chewed his lower lip savagely. At last darkly: "Gosseyn, it's unheard of. There's never been anything like it in the history of the galaxy. Conquered people or nations, even whole planetary groups, remain at home and the great mass always submits. They may hate the conqueror for a few generations, but if the propaganda is handled right, soon they take pride in their membership in a great empire." He shrugged, muttered half to himself, "The tactics are routine."

Gosseyn was thinking, "Ten million Venusian casualties in less than four days." The figure was so enormous that he closed his eyes. Slowly, then, and grimly, he opened them again. He felt a great pride and a great sorrow. The philosophy of null-A was justified, proved, honored by its dead. As one man, Venusians had realized the situation, and without agreement, with no pre-planning or warning, had done what was necessary. It was a victory for sanity that would surely leave its impress on every thoughtful man in the universe. Out there on the planets of other stars, men of good will must exist in very large numbers.

Gosseyn made an automatic estimate of how many billions of honest men there would be. The figures startled him, altered the flow of his thought. He stared at Thorson with narrowed eyes.

"Just a moment," he said slowly. "What are you trying to put over? How could a galactic empire with more soldiers than there are people in the solar system be defeated in four days? Why shouldn't they be able to supply virtually endless armies and if necessary exterminate every null-A on Venus?"

The expression on Thorson's face was sardonic. "That," he said, "was what I was talking about a little while ago."

Without taking his gaze from Gosseyn's face, the big man drew up a chair and sat down astride it, leaning his elbows on the back. There was an intentness in his manner that left no doubt of the importance of what he was about to say. He spoke finally, softly.

"My friend, think of it this way. The Greatest Empire—that is a literal translation, by the way, of the original word—is a member of a Galactic League. The other members outnumber us three to one, but we are the largest single power that has ever existed in time and space. Nevertheless, because of our League obligations, we can act only within certain limitations. We are signatories to treaties which *forbid* the use of a Distorter as we used it against the Machine. The treaties forbid the use of atomic energy except as a source of power and for a few other specified purposes. We destroyed the Machine with atomic torpedoes. True, they were very small ones, but atomic nonetheless. In the League lexicon, the greatest crime of all is genocide. If you kill five per cent of a population, that's war. If you kill ten per cent, that's slaughter, and subject to indemnities if you are convicted before the

160

League. If you kill twenty per cent or twenty million, whichever is the greater, that is genocide. If that is proved against you, the government of the power involved is declared outlaw, and all those responsible have to be delivered to the League for trial and execution, if convicted. An automatic state of war exists until the terms have been carried out."

Thorson paused, a humorless smile on his face. Jerkily he climbed to his feet and paced the floor. He stopped finally.

"Perhaps you are beginning to realize the problem that the Venusians have created for us here. In another week, if we continue fighting, we will all be subject to extreme penalties, with an alternative of war on the vastest scale."

His smile became grimmer. "Naturally," he said, "we shall continue the war until *I* see my way clear in this situation. And that, my friend, is where you come in."

The problem of himself came to the fore again as swiftly as that.

Gosseyn sank slowly back into his chair. He was puzzled, but he was suffering an emotional reaction that prevented thought. His body ached with anger and hatred for the galactic empire that was playing the game of power politics with human lives. He felt a consuming need to give of himself, to share in the great sacrifice that had been made, to offer his life as freely as others had offered theirs. The desire to be at one with the people of Venus was almost overpowering.

Almost. Consciously, cortically, he drew away from that death impulse. What was right for them was not necessarily right for him. It was the very essence of null-A that no two situations were the same. He was Gilbert Gosseyn II, possessor of the only extra brain in the universe. His purpose must be to remain alive and develop his special mind.

And that was what was puzzling here. Theoretically, there was no chance at all for a prisoner to accomplish any purpose of his own. But Thorson's very frankness seemed to offer hope.

Whatever it was, he would have to accept it and somehow turn it to his own advantage.

He saw that Thorson was still staring down at him, a

somber expression on his face now. The big man said slowly, "What I don't understand, Gosseyn, is where do *you* fit into this picture?"

He looked puzzled. "You were shoved onto the scene, almost literally, on the eve of the attack. Ostensibly, your appearance was designed to stop the invasion. I admit you delayed us, but not for long. In the final issue you seem to have served no useful purpose. The attack has been defeated not because of anything you did but because of the philosophy of a race."

He stopped. His head tilted very sharply to the right in an unconscious but expressive hesitation. He seemed absorbed in the problem at hand. When he spoke again, his voice was husky.

"And yet—and yet, there must be a connection. Gosseyn, how do you explain the co-existence of unique null-A and unique you in an otherwise ordinary universe? Wait! Don't answer! Let me show you the picture as I see it. First, we gave you death, not because we particularly wanted to, but because it seemed easier to kill you when you escaped than to bother with you. That was bad. Even thinking in such terms showed on what a narrow basis we were making our identifications.

"When Prescott reported that you had reappeared on Venus, at first I refused to believe it. I ordered Crang to find you, and then, because I wanted your co-operation, I had Prescott play that little game of appearing to help you escape. It provided an opportunity for getting rid of Lavoisseur and Hardie, and through Dr Kair we found out something about your extra brain. You will have to forgive our methods because we were so upset when you appeared in a second body.

"Immortality!" He was leaning forward, his eyes slightly distended, as if he were re-experiencing an emotion that had rocked the foundations of his being. He seemed unaware that he had given away "X's" real name. Lavoisseur! Gosseyn recalled having heard the name somewhere, but the connection was vague. Thorson went on, "Somebody had discovered the secret of human immortality. An immortality that is proof even against accidents. That is"—he paused contemptuously—"except the kind of accidents that can happen to bodies on Earth,

162

where outsiders and their weapons have access everywhere."

Thorson paused, and looked keenly at Gosseyn. "You'll be interested to know where we found the body of Gosseyn III. Frankly, I was always a little suspicious of Lavoisseur. Just because he had that accident, I didn't quite see him turning against his old work and joining up with the enemies of null-A. So I paid a visit to the Semantic building on Korzybski Square and—"

He stopped again, tantalizingly, this time. And Gosseyn gasped, "It was *there?*" He didn't wait for the answer. His mind had leaped on, beyond those words, to a new comprehension. "Lavoisseur!" he said. "I didn't get the name before. You mean 'X' was Lavoisseur, head of the Semantics Institute?"

"His accident was publicized two years ago when it happened," said Thorson. "Very few people knew how bad it had been. But that's unimportant now. What matters is, there was your third body. The scientists in charge swore it was brought in only a week before and that it was supposed to be held for the Games Machine. They said they'd called the Machine in a routine fashion and verified that it would send a truck for it in a week or so. But when I found it, it was still in its case. I didn't intend to destroy the body but when my men tried to get it out of its—container, the damned thing blew up."

He pulled up the chair again, and sank into it heavily. He seemed unaware of the action, for he did not take his gaze from Gosseyn's face. He said in a ringing voice, "That's the picture, my friend. I assure you there *was* a Gosseyn III. I saw him with my own eyes, and he looked exactly like you and exactly like Gosseyn I. Seeing that third body of yours decided me to take the great personal gamble of my career."

The statement seemed to relieve him, as if by putting his decision into words he had made it final. Thorson shifted in his chair, and leaned confidentially closer.

"Gosseyn, I don't know just how much you know. I have assumed, a great deal." He added ironically, "I have not been blind to the eagerness with which other people for reasons of their own have given you information. However, they don't count." He waved his right hand with a large gesture that dismissed others with finality. "Gosseyn, what I told you a moment ago about League regulations is true enough. But, as you have probably guessed, all that doesn't matter." He paused, nevertheless, with the air of a man about to reveal a secret. *"Those treaties were deliberately broken."* He planted his feet solidly on the floor. He said darkly, "Enro is weary of the vaporings of the League. He wants war on the largest scale, and he has specifically given me instructions to exterminate the people of null-A Venus as a deliberate provocation."

He finished quietly, "Because of you I have decided not to carry out his orders."

Gosseyn had mentally watched it coming. From his first words, the big man had concentrated on the mystery of Gilbert Gosseyn. His own problem, his own duties had been incidentally brought in for purposes of clarification and explanation. And the tremendous, the almost incredible thing was that, unknowingly, Thorson had at last provided a reason for the appearance of so many Gosseyns on this vast canvas of events. The leader of an irresistible war mechanism, geared for unlimited destruction, had been turned aside from his purpose. His mind's eye was focused beyond the normal realities of his life, and the vision of immortality on which he gazed blinded him to all else. There were still loose ends, still blurs in that picture—but it was to divert this man from his goal that Gosseyn had been brought back to life. There was no doubt, either, as to where Thorson's logic was taking him.

"Gosseyn, we've got to find the cosmic chess player. Yes, I said 'we.' Whether you realize it or not, you have to be in on this search. The reasons are weighty, both personal and general. It cannot have escaped you that you're only a pawn, an incomplete version of the original. No matter how much you develop, you can probably never know who you are and what is the real purpose of the person behind you. And, Gosseyn, you must realize that he was only temporarily caught off base. Wherever he gets these additional bodies, you can be sure that he needs you for a short time only while he puts others into—production. It sounds inhuman, I know, but there's no point in fooling yourself. Whatever you do now, whatever success you attain, in a very short time you'll be scheduled for the scrap pile. And because of the accident that happened to Gosseyn III, it just may be that the life memories of I and II will be lost."

The big man's face was a study in calculation, in a tensed anticipation of action about to be taken. He said in a harsh voice, "Naturally, I am prepared to pay a price for your assistance. I won't destroy null-A. I will use no atomic energy. I break with Enro, or at least keep him in the dark as long as possible. I fight a holding war here only, and restrict the slaughter. All that I am prepared to pay for your voluntary co-operation. If we have to force your help, then I am not bound. The only question, accordingly, that remains is"—the gray-green eyes were like burning pools—"are you going to help us willingly or unwillingly? Help us you shall!"

Because of his realization of what was coming, Gosseyn had had time to decide, and time to think of some of the implications. He said now without hesitation, "Willingly, of course. But I hope you realize the initial step *must* be to train my extra brain. Are you prepared to carry your logic to that limit?"

Thorson was on his feet. He came over and patted Gosseyn on the shoulder. "I'm way ahead of you," he said in a ringing voice. "Listen, we've rigged up a transporter system between here and Earth. Crang should be here any minute with Dr. Kair. Prescott won't be here till tomorrow, because he's to be in charge on Venus, and so for the benefit of our Earth supporters he had to come by spaceship. But—"

There was a knock on the door. It opened and Dr. Kair came in, followed by Crang. Thorson waved at them, and Gosseyn stood up and a moment later silently shook hands with the psychiatrist. He was aware of Thorson and Crang talking together in low tones. Then the big man walked over to the door.

"I'll leave you three to talk over the details at your leisure. Crang tells me there's a major revolution started on Earth, so I've got to get back to the palace to direct the fighting."

The door closed behind him.

XXX

In the elder days of Art, Builders wrought with
greatest care Each minute and unseen part, For the
Gods see everywhere.

W.W.L.

"It will be," said Dr. Kair, "a battle of wits. And I'll bet
on the extra brain."

They had been talking for more than an hour, with
Crang interjecting only an occasional remark. Gosseyn
watched the hazel-eyed man from the corner of his eyes,
puzzled and uncertain. According to Kair, it was Crang
who had found and arrested him. The man, of course, had
to appear to be a Thorson man, but he was acting out his
role the hard way. Gosseyn decided not to ask him about
Patricia Hardie. Not yet, anyway. He saw that Kair was
standing up.

"No use wasting time," the psychiatrist said. "I understand that galactic technicians have been rigging up a special room for you. The training should not be difficult
with all the equipment they have here." He shook his head
wonderingly. "It's still hard for me to grasp that they've
got several square miles of underground buildings here,
with only Crang's tree house as a front. But to get back to
what I was saying." He frowned thoughtfully. "The main
point is, if we're right, your extra brain is an *organic*
Distorter, and all that that implies. With the help of the
mechanical Distorter, you should be able to similarize two
small blocks of wood in three or four days, and that will
be the beginning."

But it took only two days.

Afterward, alone in the dark room, where the test had
taken place, Gosseyn sat and stared down at the blocks.
They had been three centimeters apart. He had seen no
movement, but now they were touching. The single beam
of light that focused on the two blocks marked their
changed positions unmistakably. In some way, though he
had had no sensation, thought waves had reached out
from his extra brain and controlled matter.

The ascendancy of mind over matter—age-old dream of man. Not that he had done it without assistance. Every effort had been made to make the two blocks similar. And yet they would have changed slightly since then. So slightly. His body heat in the confined room would have affected them. Both the light beam and the surrounding darkness would have had a different influence on each block, despite the absorber tubes that lined the walls, despite the most delicate electron thermostat. Without the Distorter, of course, he wouldn't have succeeded this first time. It had similarized the blocks to nineteen decimal places. It quieted the molecular movement of the air, partially similarized the table on which the blocks rested, Gosseyn's chair, and Gosseyn himself.

And yet the final impulse had come from him. It *was* the beginning.

Gosseyn emerged from the training room, and Thorson came by transporter from Earth to assist Kair with the tests. The photographs showed thousands of tiny impulse lines that had reached up into the extra brain.

The tests were prolonged, and it was an exhausted Gosseyn who finally set out for his apartment. As he walked toward the "elevator" he noticed that, in addition to his usual guards, a small metal ball bristling with electronic tubes floated in the air behind him. Prescott, in charge of the guards, caught his glance.

"It contains a vibrator," he explained coolly. "Crang reported Kair's statement that this would be a battle of wits and we're taking no chances. It will be used to make tiny changes in the atomic structure of the walls, ceilings, floors, ground, everything—wherever you've been. It will follow you from now on right to your apartment door."

His voice grew louder. "It is a precaution against the time when you will be able to transport yourself from your apartment to any piece of matter, the structure of which you have previously 'memorized.' "

Gosseyn did not answer. He had never bothered to conceal his dislike of Prescott, and now he merely gazed at him with steady eyes. The man shrugged, but there was a significant note in his voice as he looked at his watch and said with a twisted smile, "It is our purpose, Gosseyn, to tie you down with every means available to us. To that end we have prepared a little surprise for you."

Gosseyn was still wondering about the surprise a few minutes later when he switched on the lights of his living room. He put on his pajamas and headed for the dark alcove where the beds were. A movement on one of the enshadowed pillows stopped him. A pair of sleepy eyes stared at him. Even in that dimness Gosseyn recognized the face instantly. The girl sat up with an indolent grace, and yawned.

"You and I do get around, don't we?" said Patricia Hardie.

XXXI

Gosseyn sat down on the other bed with an abrupt movement. His relief was tremendous, but when his excitement faded he recalled what Prescott had said. He said slowly, "I suppose if I try to escape, you get killed."

She nodded, more seriously. "Something like that." She added, "It was Mr. Crang's idea."

Gosseyn lay down on his bed and stared silently up at the ceiling. Crang again. His doubts about the man began to dissolve. He wondered if Thorson had wanted to kill Patricia and if this was Crang's compromise suggestion for saving her life without having to come out into the open himself. He could almost visualize the man pointing out to Thorson that Gilbert Gosseyn had once believed himself to be married to Patricia Hardie and that some of the emotion might have remained. It could be one more tie to hold him to his bargain. So Crang might have argued.

Brilliant Eldred Crang, thought Gosseyn. The one man in all this affair who had so far not made a personal mistake. From the corner of his eye, he glanced at Patricia. She was yawning and stretching like a relaxed kitten. She turned her head and caught his gaze.

"Haven't you any questions to ask?" she said.

He pondered that. He couldn't ask about Crang, of course. And he had no idea how much she had confessed to Thorson. It wouldn't do to talk about things of which Thorson knew nothing. Gosseyn said cautiously, "I think I know the whole situation fairly well. We on Earth and

Venus have witnessed a greedy interstellar empire trying to take over another planetary system, in spite of the disapproval of a purely Aristotelian league. It's all very childish and murderous, an extreme example of how neurotic a civilization can become when it fails to develop a method for integrating the human part of man's mind with the animal part. All their thousands of years of additional scientific development have been wasted in the effort to achieve size and power when all they needed was to learn how to co-operate. Yes, I have a fairly good over-all picture. The status of certain individuals still puzzles me. You."

"I'm your wife," said the woman. And Gosseyn was irritated that she should joke at such a time.

"Don't you think," he said reproachfully, "it's unwise to make vital admissions? Eavesdroppers might—well, you know."

She laughed softly, then said earnestly, "My friend, Thorson is being led around by the nose by the sharpest-brained man I've ever met. Eldred Crang. I assure you Eldred has seen to it that we can talk freely."

Gosseyn let that go. There was no doubt about her admiration for her lover. The woman went on slowly, "I don't know just how long Eldred can go on as he has been, or how long he can protect us. Thorson will kill us when it suits his purpose, as casually and callously as he did my father and 'X.' If the person behind you fails us, then we are all as good as dead right now."

Her conviction upset Gosseyn for an odd reason. She clearly had no faith in anything he might do. Was it possible that they were all depending on an individual who had not once come into the open? Didn't Crang have any solution for the day when the extra brain was finally trained? He asked the question.

"Eldred has no plans," said Patricia Hardie. "At that point you go on your own."

Gosseyn turned out the light. "Patricia," he said into the darkness, "do you think I've made a mistake in agreeing to Thorson's plan?"

"I don't know."

"We'll find this mysterious person, I'm pretty sure."

She hesitated, then, "Eldred thinks so too."

Eldred again. Damn Eldred.

"Why didn't Crang warn your father?"

"He didn't know what was being planned."

"You mean, Thorson suspects him?"

"No. But 'X' was a Crang man. Thorson obviously thought Crang would oppose his elimination, and so he worked the assassination through Prescott."

Gosseyn said softly, " 'X' was a Crang man?"

"Yes."

It was hard to imagine that, much easier to believe the monstrosity had been turned into an egocentric by his injuries. And yet even Thorson had been suspicious of "X."

"It seems to me," Gosseyn said at last sourly, "that the entire structure of the opposition to Enro is built on the machinations of Eldred Crang." He stopped. Putting the thought into words made the man seem bigger than life. Gosseyn's mind made a tremendous leap. "Is *he* the cosmic chess player?"

Patricia's answer came instantly. "Definitely not."

"What makes you say that?"

"He has pictures of himself when he was a child."

"Pictures could be faked." Swiftly.

She didn't reply to that, and after a moment Gosseyn abandoned the subject of Crang. "What about your father?"

"My father," she said quietly, "believed the Machine had wrongly denied him advancement in spite of his qualifications. When I was a child, I shared his resentment. I refused to have anything to do with null-A. But he went too far for me. When I began to realize that behind his wonderful personality—and you must admit he had it—was a man who felt careless of the consequences of his acts, I secretly rebelled. When Eldred came on the scene a year and a half ago, after a meteoric rise in the diplomatic service of the Greatest Empire, I had my first contact with the Galactic League."

"He's a galactic agent?"

"No." There was pride in her voice. "Eldred Crang is Eldred Crang, unique individual. He put me in touch with the League."

"And you became a League agent?"

"In my own way."

There was a tone to her voice that made Gosseyn say quickly, "What do you mean by that?"

"The League," said Patricia, "suffers from many shortcomings. It's only as determined as its member nations. It's so easy, so awfully easy, to sacrifice one star system for the good of the whole. I always kept that in mind, and so worked *for* Earth *through* the League. The permanent League personnel," she added, "has long been aware of null-A, but has been unable to promote it anywhere else in the galaxy. The various governments associate it with pacifism, which it is not. They cannot imagine a state where the people adjust instantly to the requirements of any situation, including extreme militarism."

Gosseyn nodded, remembering what Thorson had told him. He ceased wondering why Enro had chosen an obscure planetary system in which to provoke his war. An attack on the only unarmed planet in the galaxy would be the most brazen method of flouting the League treaties.

"It was Eldred," said Patricia, "who discovered that the injuries suffered by old Lavoisseur in the explosion at the Semantics Institute a few years ago had turned that great scientist into the bloodthirsty maniac whom you knew as 'X.' He thought the man would recover, and so become useful, but that didn't happen."

Back to Eldred. Gosseyn sighed.

The silence between them lengthened. With each passing minute, Gosseyn grew more determined, grimmer. He had no illusions. This was the calm before the storm. A rapacious Thorson had been drawn from the purpose for which he had come to the solar system. So the world of null-A had a chance to arm itself, and the League had a few additional weeks to realize that Enro meant war. Thorson would play his private game as long as he dared, but if he ever felt himself threatened, he would carry on with the war of extermination.

Gosseyn could see his hopes narrowing down to one lone being working, with the help of a few uncomprehending assistants like himself, against the colossal might of a violently *un*sane, all-embracing galactic civilization.

"It's not enough," he thought with sudden insight. "I'm

171

counting too much on somebody else to perform the final miracle."

In that moment, with that realization, the first germ of desperate action was born.

XXXII

Two days after that, he bent two light beams together in the dark room without the aid of the Distorter. He felt the action. Felt it as a sensation like—he tried to describe it afterward to the others—like "the first time you get a floating arm in hypnosis." Distinct, unmistakable attunement. It was a new awareness of—and addition to—his nervous system.

As the days passed, the tingles in his body grew more insistent, sharper, and more controllable. He felt energies, movements, things, and reached the point where he could identify them instantly. The presence of the other men was a warm fire along his nerves. He responded to the most delicate impulses, and by the sixth day he could distinguish Dr. Kair from the others by a "friendliness" that effused from the man. There was an overtone of anxiety in the psychologist's feeling, but that only accentuated the friendliness.

Gosseyn was interested in distinguishing between the emotions felt about him by Crang, Prescott, and Thorson. It was Prescott who disliked him violently. "He's never forgotten," Gosseyn thought, "the scare I gave him, and the way I fooled him again when I went to the palace to get the Distorter." Thorson was a Machiavellian; he neither liked nor disliked his prisoner. He was both cautious and resolute. Crang was neutral. It was a curious emotion to receive from the man. Neutral, intent, preoccupied, playing a game so intricate that no clear-cut reaction would come through.

But it was Patricia who provided the startling state. Nothing. Again and again, when he reached the point where he could identify the individual emotions of the men, Gosseyn strained to make contact with Patricia's nervous system. In the end he had to conclude that a man could not tune in on a woman.

During those days his plan grew sharper in his mind. He saw with a developing comprehension that the picture of this situation had come to him through Aristotelian minds—almost literally. Even Crang, he mustn't forget, was only a fine example of how man could organize himself without having had knowledge of the null-A system since childhood. He was a null-A convert, and not a null-A proper.

There were gaps in that reasoning, but it brought the scene down to the level of a human nervous system. The mysterious player, seen in that light, no longer seemed so important. He was a concept of Thorson's Aristotelian mind. The reality would probably turn out to be some one who had discovered a method of immortality, and who was attempting without adequate resources to oppose the plans of an irresistible military power. He had already proved that he cared little about what happened to any one body of Gilbert Gosseyn, and it seemed clear that if Gosseyn II was killed, then the player would accept the defeat of that phase of his plans and turn to other prospects of the situation.

To hell with him!

On the afternoon of the experiment with the piece of wood, Gosseyn made a prolonged attempt to counteract the vibrator. Its intricacy startled him. It was a thing of many subtly different energies. Pulsations poured from it on a multitude of wave lengths. He succeeded in controlling it because it was a small machine, its various parts close together in space-time. The time difference between the innumerable functions was not a factor.

And that was why his control of it meant nothing so far as his escape was concerned. The time factor *was* important when, holding the vibrator, he tried simultaneously to memorize the structure of a section of the floor. He couldn't dominate both. That situation continued. He could control the vibrator *or* the floor, never the two of them together. The gang knew its Similarity science; that was finally clear.

On the nineteenth day he was given a metal rod with a concave cup made of electron steel, the metal used for atomic energy. Gingerly, Gosseyn reached with his mind for the small electric power source that had been brought into the room. The sparkling force coruscated in the energy cup and spat with a hazy violence against the floor, the wall, the transparent shield behind which the observers waited. Shuddering, Gosseyn broke the twenty-decimal similarity between the rod and the energy source. He surrendered the rod to a soldier who was sent out to take it from him. Not till then did Thorson come out. The big man was genial.

"Well, Mr. Gosseyn," he said, almost respectfully, "we'd be foolish to give you any more training than that. It isn't that I don't trust you—" He laughed. "I don't. But I think you've got enough stuff to find our man."

He broke off. "I'm having some extra clothing sent up to your apartment. Pack what you want, and be ready in an hour."

Gosseyn nodded absently. A few moments later he watched the three guards ease the vibrator into the elevator, and then Prescott motioned him to enter. The men crowded in behind him. Prescott stepped to the controls, and Gosseyn, in a single, convulsive movement, grabbed him and smashed his head against the metal wall of the elevator. Even as he snatched at the blaster in the holster strapped to the man's hip, he let go of the body, reached for the nearest tube, and pressed it.

There was a blur of movement; that ended. By that time the blaster was glaring its white fire, and there were four dying men writhing on the floor.

The tremendous, desperate first act was a complete success.

XXXIII

Gosseyn tugged open the zippers and peeled off his suit. He suspected that electronic instruments were woven into its cloth, and there was at least one such device by which the wearer could be stunned by remote control. Stripped, he began to feel better, but it was not until he had hastily donned Prescott's suit and shoes that he considered himself ready for the next move.

He opened the elevator door and glanced along the unfamiliar corridor onto which it opened. He wondered briefly just where his chance pressure on the control tube had brought him. It didn't matter where he was, of course. This first stop had one purpose only—to get rid of the vibrator.

He shoved it unceremoniously out, and bundled the four bodies after it pitilessly. There was a door a score of feet along the hallway, but he had no time for exploration. This was one level that he must not come back to, for here the vibrator could nullify all his hopes; he just didn't have the time to examine it and shut off its interfering pulsations. Back in the elevator, he pressed a tube that took him to another unfamiliar corridor. Like the first one, it was empty. Gosseyn "memorized" the pattern of part of the floor near the elevator shafts and gave to its pattern the key number, one. At top speed he raced a hundred yards along the corridor, and paused when he came to a turn in the corridor. Just around the corner, he "memorized" a pattern of a small section of the floor, and gave it the key letter, A. Standing there, he thought, "One!"

Instantly he was back at the elevator shaft.

The sense of triumph that leaped through him was like nothing else he had ever experienced. He darted back into the elevator and pressed a third tube. The key words on that corridor were "2" and "B," respectively. . . . As he stepped out of the elevator on the fourth corridor, a man was just coming out of the elevator in the next shaft. Remorselessly, Gosseyn opened up on him with his arsenal of weapons. He shoved the smoldering, twitching thing back into the elevator from which it had emerged a moment before.

That was the only incident of his swift progression. And yet, in spite of his speed, though he did not pause once to so much as glance inside a door, he estimated that half an hour had gone by when he finally reached the goal he had set himself: Nine pattern keys and as far as "I" in the alphabet of alternative patterns. And every electric socket on the way was "memorized" by a system of mathematical symbols.

He stepped back into the elevator and pressed the tube that took him to the corridor that led to Patricia's and his apartment. It too showed no sign that his break had yet been discovered. Gosseyn paused before the closed door, and made another brief survey of his situation. It was not absolutely perfect, but he had eighteen places to which he could retreat, and forty-one sources of energy on which his extra brain could draw. He saw that his hands were trembling the slightest bit, and he felt as if he had been perspiring. A natural tension, he decided. He was keyed up. In less than thirty minutes, he would be launched on the greatest military campaign ever attempted by one man, at least in his knowledge. In an hour he would be victorious or he would be dead forever.

His mental summation completed, he turned the knob and opened the door. Patricia Hardie leaped out of a chair and raced across the rug toward him. "For heavens sake," she breathed, "where have you been?"

She broke off. "But never mind that. Eldred was here."

There was nothing in her voice to indicate that she knew what had happened. Yet her words shocked Gosseyn. He had his first inkling of what she was going to say.

"Crang!" He spoke the name as if it were a bomb he was handling.

"He brought final instructions."

"My God!" said Gosseyn.

He felt weak. He had waited and waited for some word. He had deliberately delayed until the last possible hour before he acted. And now this. The woman seemed unaware of his reaction.

"He said"—her voice sank to a whisper—"he said for you to pretend to be drawn to the Semantics building, and there co-operate with—with—" She swayed as if she were about to faint.

Gosseyn caught her, held her up. "Yes. Yes. With whom?"

"A bearded man!" It was a sigh. She straightened slowly, but she was trembling. "It's hard to imagine that Eldred has known about—him all this time."

"But who is he?"

"Eldred didn't say."

The anger that came to Gosseyn was all the more violent because what she was saying meant nothing after the irrevocable things he had done. But with all his strength and all his will he held that fury down. Patricia mustn't suspect yet what had happened, not until she had given him every bit of information that she had.

"What's the plan?" he said, and this time it was he who whispered.

"Death for Thorson."

That was obvious. "Yes, yes?" Gosseyn urged.

"Then Eldred will have control of the army that Thorson brought with him. That's been the difficulty." She spoke hurriedly. "Thorson commands a hundred million men in this sector of the galaxy. If those men can be gotten from Enro, it will take a year or more to organize another attack on Venus."

Gosseyn let go of the girl and sagged into a near-by chair. The logic was dazzling. His own plan had been simply to try to kill Thorson, but failing that—and he expected to fail—he intended trying to destroy the base. It was a good stopgap scheme, but it was a tiny hope compared to the vaster scheme of Crang. No wonder the man had compromised with murder if this was the ending he had in mind. Patricia was speaking again.

"Eldred says Thorson cannot be killed here in the base. There are too many protective devices. He's got to be led out where he is not so well protected."

Gosseyn nodded warily. In its own way it sounded as dangerous as what he had done. And as vague. He was to co-operate with a bearded man. He looked up.

"Is that all Crang said—co-operation?"

"That's all."

They expected a great deal, Gosseyn thought bitterly. Once more he was supposed to follow blindly the ideas of another person. If he surrendered now, or pretended to be captured—he could see how he might do that with a certain cunning—it would mean giving up every gain, submitting to even closer supervision, and accepting the hope that some unknown plan of the bearded man would work. If only he knew the identity of even one of the people whose instructions he was following. The thought gave him pause.

"Patricia, who is Crang?"

She looked at him. "Don't you know? Haven't you guessed?"

"Twice," Gosseyn said, "a suspicion has jumped into my

mind, but I couldn't see how he would have worked it. It seems fairly clear that if the galactic civilization can produce a man like that, then we'd better give up null-A and adopt their educational system."

"It's really very simple," the woman said quietly. "Five years ago, in the course of his practice on Venus, he grew suspicious of the null-A pretensions of a man who worked on a case with him. The man, as you might guess, was an agent of Prescott. That was his first inkling of the galactic plot. Even at that time, a warning would only have forced Enro to make a quick decision, and of course Eldred had no idea just what was being planned. He took it for granted others would discover what he had learned, and so he merely tried to cover his own trail. He spent the next few years out in space working his way up in the service of the Greatest Empire. Naturally, he adjusted to every necessity of the situation. He told me he had to kill a hundred and thirty-seven men to get to the top. He regards what he is doing as in the normal line of duty, and quite average—"

"Average!" Gosseyn exploded. And then he subsided. He had his answer. Eldred Crang, an *average* Venusian null-A detective, had suggested a course of action. His method was not necessarily the best one, but it was undoubtedly based on more information than was possessed by Gilbert Gosseyn. Part of its purpose—to bring the mysterious player out into the open—would compensate to some extent for the sorry ending of what he had started with such boldness.

He'd pretend to fight, but would permit a quick capture. There'd probably be some bad moments, particularly if they questioned him with a lie detector. But that was a chance he had to take. Fortunately, lie detectors never volunteered information. Still, if the wrong question were asked, then Crang might have to act fast.

During the battle that followed, Gosseyn retreated in turn to the nine *numbered* patterns, leaving the *lettered* ones as a reserve in case the wrong questions were asked. There was just enough confusion involved—a numbered and a lettered pattern on each floor—to justify the hope that he could keep his secrets. He ended up on the corridor of pattern "7." There, pretending he had come to the end of his resources, he burned out a wall by short-circuiting the electricity, and then let himself be captured.

He had to tense every muscle in his body to restrain his relief when he saw that the questioner before whom he was taken was Eldred Crang. The interview that followed seemed thorough. But so carefully were the questions worded that not once did the lie detector give away any vital fact. When it was finally over, Crang turned to a wall receiver and said, "I think, Mr. Thorson, you can safely take him to Earth. Everything here will be taken care of."

Gosseyn had been wondering where Thorson was. It was clear that the man was taking no unnecessary chances—and yet Thorson had to go to Earth personally. That was the beauty of all this. The search for the secret of immortality could not be delegated to subordinates whose life-hunger might cause them, also, to forget their duty.

The big man was standing beside a row of elevators when Gosseyn was brought up. His manner was condescending.

"It's as I thought," he said. "This extra brain of yours has its limitations. After all, if it was able to oppose a major invasion by itself, then the third Gosseyn would have been brought out without preliminaries. The truth is, one man is always vulnerable. Even with a limited immortality, and a few bodies to play around with, he can do very little more than any bold man. His enemies need merely suspect his whereabouts and an atomic bomb could wipe out everything in that vicinty before he could so much as think."

He waved his hand. "We'll forget about Prescott. Fact is, I'm rather pleased that this happened. It puts things in their proper perspective. The fact that you tried it, though, shows that you've thoroughly misunderstood my motives." He shrugged. "We're not going to kill this player, Gosseyn. We merely want to participate in what he's got."

Gosseyn said nothing, but he knew better. It was the nature of Aristotelian man that he did not share willingly. All through history the struggle for power, murder of rivals, and exploitation of the defenseless had been the reality of unintegrated man's nature. Julius Caesar and Pompey refusing to share the Roman Empire, Napoleon, first an honest defender of his country then a restless conqueror—such men were the spiritual forebears of Enro, who would not share the galaxy. Even now, as Thorson sat here denying ambition, his brain must be roiling with schemes and visions of colossal destiny. Gosseyn was glad when the giant said, "And now let's go. We've wasted enough time."

It was something to be up and going toward the crisis.

XXXIV

"What you say a thing is, it is not" . . . It is much more. It is a compound in the largest sense. A chair is not just a chair. It is a structure of inconceivable complexity, chemically, atomically, electronically, etc. Therefore, to think of it simply as a chair is to confine the nervous system to what Korzybski calls an identification. It is the totality of such identifications that create the neurotic, the unsane, and the insane individual.

Anonymous

The city of the Machine was changed. There had been fighting, and smashed buildings were everywhere. When they came to the palace, Gosseyn was no longer surprised that Thorson had spent the previous few days on Venus.

The palace was a shattered, empty husk. Gosseyn wandered with the others along its bare corridors and through its smashed rooms with a nostalgic sense of a civilization going down and down. The firing in the distant streets was a throbbing background to his movements, a continuous, unpleasant mutter, irritating, polysonal. Thorson answered his question curtly. "They're just as bad here as on Venus. They fight like mindless fiends."

"It's a level of abstraction in the null-A sense," Gosseyn said matter of factly. "Complete adjustment to the necessities of the situation."

Thorson said, "Aaaaaa!" in any annoyed tone, then changed the subject. "Do you feel anything?"

Gosseyn shook his head truthfully. "Nothing."

They came to Patricia's room. The wall where the Distorter had been gaped at them. The French windows lay shattered on the floor. Through the empty frames, Gosseyn stared out toward where the Games Machine had once towered like a jewel crowning the green Earth. Where it had been, thousands and thousands of truckloads of soil had been dumped, perhaps with the intention of leveling all traces of the symbol of a World's struggle for sanity. Only, no leveler was at work. The unsightly earth lay multitudinously humped and seemingly forgotten.

They could find no clue in the palace, and presently the whole mass of men and machines headed for Dan Lyttle's house. It stood untouched. Automatics had kept it spic and span; the rooms smelled as fresh and clean as he had left them. The crate that had contained the Distorter stood in one corner of the living room. The address, "The Semantics Institute," to which the Games Machine had intended it to be sent, was huge on the side that faced the room. Gosseyn motioned toward it, as if suddenly struck by a thought.

"Why not there?"

An armored army moved along the streets of what had been the city of the Machine. Fleets of roboplanes rode the skies. Above them spaceships hovered, ready for anything. Robotanks and fast cars swarmed along all near-by streets. They raced in silent processions into the famous square, and then men and machines poured into the buildings through the doors from every direction. At the many-doored ornamental entrance, Thorson indicated the letters carved in the marble. Somberly, Gosseyn paused, and read the ancient inscription:

THE NEGATIVE JUDGMENT

IS THE PEAK OF MENTALITY

It was like a sigh across the centuries. Some of the reality of meaning, as it affected the human nervous system, was in that phrase. Countless billions of people had lived and died without ever suspecting that their positive beliefs had helped to create the disordered brains with which they confronted the realities of their worlds.

Men in uniforms emerged from the nearest entrance. One of them spoke to Thorson in a language heavy with consonants. The big man turned to Gosseyn.

"It's deserted," he said.

Gosseyn did not answer. Deserted. The word echoed along the corridors of his mind. The Semantics building deserted. He might have guessed, of course, that it would be. The men in charge were only human, and they could not be expected to live in the no man's land between two fighting forces. But still he hadn't expected it.

He grew aware that Thorson was speaking to the men operating the vibrator. Its pulsations, which had been briefly silent, crept in upon him. Thorson turned to him again.

"We'll turn the vibrator off again when we get inside. I'm not taking any chances with you."

Gosseyn roused himself. "We're going inside?"

"We'll tear the place apart," said Thorson. "There may be hidden rooms."

He began to shout orders. There was a period of confusion. Men kept coming out of the building and reporting to the big man. They spoke in the same incomprehensible, guttural language, and it was not until Thorson turned to him with a grim smile that he had any inkling of what was happening.

"They've found an old man working in one of the laboratories. They can't understand how they missed him before but"—he waved an arm impatiently—"that doesn't matter. I told them to leave him alone while I figure this out."

Gosseyn did not doubt the translation. Thorson was pale. For more than a minute, the big man stood with a black frown on his face. At last:

"This is one chance I'm not taking," he said. "We'll go inside, but . . ."

They climbed the fourteen-carat gold steps and passed the jewel-inlaid platinum doors and into the massive anteroom, with its millions of diamonds set into every square inch of the high walls and domed ceiling. The effect was so dazzling that it struck Gosseyn the original builders had overreached themselves. The structure had been put up at a time when a great campaign was on to convince people that the so-called jewels and precious metals, so long regarded as the very essence of wealth, were actually no more valuable than other scarce materials. Even after hundreds of years, the propaganda was unconvincing.

They walked along a corridor of matched rubies, and climbed an emerald stairway that shimmered with green iridescence. The anteroom at the head of the stairs was solid, untarnishable silver, and beyond that was a corridor of the famous and colorful plastic *opalescent*. The hallway swarmed with men, and Gosseyn had a sinking sensation. Thorson stopped and indicated a doorway a hundred feet ahead.

"He's in there."

Gosseyn stood in a mental mist. His lips parted to ask for a description of the old man who had been discovered. "Does he have a beard?" he wanted to say. But he couldn't utter a sound.

He thought in agony, "What am I supposed to do?"

Thorson nodded at Gosseyn. "I've put a blaster company in with him. They're there now, watching him. So now it's up to you. Go on in and tell him this building is surrounded, and that our instruments show no source of radioactive energies, so there is nothing he can do against us."

He raised himself to his great height, and stood half a head above his prisoner. "Gosseyn," he roared, "I warn you, make no false moves. I'll destroy Earth and Venus if anything goes wrong now."

The sheer savagery of the threat struck an answering fire from Gosseyn. They glared at each other like two beasts of prey. It was Thorson who broke the tension with a laugh.

"All right, all right," he snapped, "so we're both on edge. Let's forget it. But remember, this is life or death."

His teeth clamped together with a click. "Move!" he said.

Gosseyn was cold with the cold which derives from the nervous system. Slowly he stiffened. He began to walk forward.

"Gosseyn, when you come to the alcove near the door, step into it. You'll be safe there."

Gosseyn jumped as if he had been struck. No words had been spoken, yet the thought had come into his mind as clearly as if it were his own.

"Gosseyn, every metal case along the corridors and in every room has an energy cup in it wired for thousands of volts."

There was no doubt of it now. In spite of what Prescott had once said about the necessity of establishing twenty-decimal similarity with another brain before there could be telepathy, he was receiving someone else's thoughts.

The climax had come so abruptly, so differently than he had expected, that he froze where he was. He remembered thinking, "I've got to get going! Get going!"

"Gosseyn, get into the alcove—and nullify the vibrator!"

He was already moving toward the door when that thought came. He could see the alcove ten feet away, then five; and then there was a roar from Thorson.

"Get out of that alcove! What are you trying to do?"

"Nullify the vibrator!"

He was trying. His body pulsed with silent energy as it became attuned to the vibrator. His vision blurred, then cleared as a bolt of artificial lightning sizzled past the alcove, straight at Thorson. The big man went down, his head nearly burned off, and the great fire coruscated past him down the corridor. Men screamed in agony. A fireball floated from the ceiling and engulfed the circular vibrator. It blew up in a cloud of flame, tearing to shreds the men who had been manning it and protecting it.

Instantly, the weight of vibratory pulsations cleared from Gosseyn's nerves.

"Gosseyn, hurry! Don't let them recover. Don't give them a chance to advise the planes above to bomb. I can't do it. I've been burned by a blaster. Clear the building, then come back here. Hurry! I'm badly hurt."

Hurt! In an agony of anxiety Gosseyn pictured the man dying before he could get any information from him. He snatched for a source of power—and in ten minutes wrecked the building and the square. Corridors were seared with the murderous fire he poured along them. Walls caved in on shouting men. Tanks smoldered and burned like fury. "No one"—almost like fire itself was the thought—"no one of this special guard can be allowed to get away."

Not one did. A regiment of men and machines had swarmed into the square. Torn, blackened bodies and smashed metal was all that remained. Gosseyn looked up from one of the doorways. The planes hovered at a thousand feet. Without orders from Thorson they would hesitate to bomb. Perhaps already Crang had taken them over.

He couldn't wait to make sure. Back into the building he raced, along a smoldering corridor. As he entered the laboratory, Gosseyn stopped short. The corpses of Thorson's guards sprawled in every direction. Slumped in an easy chair beside a desk was an old, bearded man. He looked up at Gosseyn with glazed eyes, mustered a smile and said, "Well, we did it!"

His voice was deep and strong and familiar. Gosseyn stared at him, remembering where he had heard that bass voice before. The shock of recognition held his own reaction down to a single word.

" 'X!' " he said loudly.

XXXV

I am the family face.
Flesh perishes, I live on,
Projecting trait and trace
Through time to times anon,
And leaping from place to place
Over oblivion.

T.H.

The old man coughed. It was not a pleasant sound, for he twisted in agony. The movement brushed aside a fold of scorched cloth and showed the blistered flesh underneath. There was a gap in his right side, high up, as big as a fist. Thick threads of blood dangled from it.

"It's all right," he mumbled. "I can pretty well hold off the pain except when I'm coughing. Self-hypnosis, you know."

He straightened stiffly. " 'X,' " he said then. "Well, yes, I suppose I am, if you want to put it that way. I put 'X' out to be my personal spy in the highest circles. But of course he didn't know it. That's the beauty of the system of immortality which I perfected. *All* the thoughts of the active body are telepathically received by other passive bodies of the same, uh, culture. Naturally, I had to disappear from the scene when he came on stage. Couldn't have two Lavoisseurs around, you know." He leaned back wearily, then with a sigh: "In 'X's case I wanted someone whose thoughts would come back to me while I was conscious, so I damaged him and speeded up his life processes. That was cruel, but it made him the 'greater' and me the 'lesser'—that way I received his thoughts. Except for that he was independent. He actually was the rogue he thought he was."

His head drooped, his eyes closed, and Gosseyn thought he had lapsed into a coma. He felt despair, for there was nothing he could do here. The player was dying, and still Gilbert Gosseyn knew nothing about himself. He thought in anguish, "I've got to force information out of him." He bent down and shook the man.

"Wake up!" he shouted.

The body stirred. The tired eyes opened, and looked at him thoughtfully. "I was trying," said the bass voice, "to operate an energy cup to kill this body. Couldn't do it. . . . You understand, it was always my intention to die the moment Thorson was dead. . . . Expected to be killed instantly when I opened my defenses. . . . Soldiers did a poor job." He shook his head. "Logical, of course. The body's the first thing that weakens, next the cortex, and then—" His eyes brightened. "Will you bring me a weapon from one of those soldiers? I'm finding it hard to fight off the pain."

Gosseyn secured a blaster, but his brain was working furiously. "Am I going to force a desperately wounded man to stay alive and suffer while I ask questions?" The conflict upset him physically, but in the end, grimly, he knew that he was. He shook his head when Lavoisseur held out his hand. The old man looked at him sharply.

"Want information, eh?" he mumbled. He laughed, a curious, amused laugh. "All right, what do you want?"

"My bodies. How—"

He was cut off. "The secret of immortality," said the old man, "involves the isolation in an individual of the

186

uplicate potentials he inherited from his parents. Like wins, or brothers who look alike. Theoretically, similarity ould be achieved in a normal birth. But actually, only nder laboratory conditions, with the bodies kept unonscious by automatic hypno drugs in an electronic inubator, can a proper environment be maintained. There, vithout any thoughts of their own, massaged by machines, ed a liquid diet, their bodies change slightly from the riginal, but their minds change only according to the houghts they receive from their alter ego, who is out in he world. In practice, a Distorter is necessary to the procss, and a lie-detector type of instrument is set to cut off ertain unnecessary thoughts—in your case nearly all houghts were blotted out, so that you wouldn't know too nuch. But because of this thought similarity, while death ctually strikes body after body, the same personality goes n."

The leonine head sagged. "That's it. That's practically ll. Crang has given you most of the reasons, directly or ndirectly. We had to divert that attack."

Gosseyn said, "The extra brain?"

The old man sighed but did not lift his head. "It exists n embryo in every normal human brain. But it can't levelop under the tensions of conscious life. Just as the cortex of George the animal boy wouldn't develop under he abnormal conditions of living with a dog, so the mere train of active existence is too much for the extra brain in he early stages. . . .It becomes very strong, of course. . . ."

He was silent, and Gosseyn gave him a moment of rest while his mind flashed over what he had been told. Duplicate potentials. It would have to be a culture of such male spermatozoa; the science involved was hundreds of years old. The development of life in incubators was even older. The rest was detail. The important thing was to find out where the bodies were kept.

He asked the question in a tensed tone, and when there was no answer, caught the old man's shoulder. At his touch the body fell limply forward. Startled, he lowered it gently to the floor. With a jerky movement, Gosseyn knelt and listened over the still heart. Slowly he climbed to his feet. And he was thinking, and his lips were forming the unspoken words: "But you didn't tell me enough. I'm in the dark about all the main points."

The thought quieted reluctantly. He realized that this was life itself he was experiencing. Life in which nothing was ever finally explained. He was free, and this was victory.

He knelt down and began to search the old man's pockets. They were empty. He was about to stand up again when:

"My God, man, give me that gun!"

Gosseyn froze, and then with a gasp realized that he had heard no sound and that he had received the thought of a dead man. Indecisively at first, then with greater determination, he began to shake the body gently. The cells of the human brain were extremely mortal, but they didn't die immediately after the heart stopped beating. If one thought had come, then others should be available. The minutes fled. It was the intricate process of dying, Gosseyn thought, that was causing the delay. It had already partially destroyed some of the similarity that Lavoisseur had established between them.

"Might as well stay alive for a while, Gosseyn. The next group of bodies are around eighteen years old. Wait till they're thirty—that's it, thirty. . . ."

That was all, but Gosseyn thrilled with excitement. He must have stimulated a tiny mass of cells. Once again, the minutes flowed by, and then: -

"—Memory certainly turned out to be a remarkable . . . But between your group and mine, the continuity was broken. My accident was too much for the process. Too bad—but, still, you've already had the experience of apparently surviving as an individual, so you know how complete—"

This time, there was only the tiniest pause, then the next thought followed:

". . . I used to wonder if there wasn't someone else. I thought of myself as a queen in the game—in such a set-up you would be a pawn on the seventh row, just about ready to queen. But then I'd come to a blank, for a queen no matter how powerful is only a piece. Who, then, is the player? Where did all this start? . . . Once more . . . (incoherently) . . . the circle is completing, and we are no further ahead—"

Frantically, Gosseyn fought to hold the connection, but there was a blur, and then nothing. As he strained for more thoughts, he grew conscious of the fantastic thing he was doing. He pictured himself in this shattered, bejeweled building trying to read the mind of a dead man. Surely, in all the universe, this was unique. The personal thought faded, because, once more—contact.

". . . Gosseyn, more than five hundred years ago . . . I nourished Null-A, which someone else started. I was looking for a place to settle, and for something to be that was more than mere continuity; and it seemed to me that the Non-Aristotelian Man was it . . . Our secret of immortality could not, of course, be given to the unintegrated, who would, like Thorson, think of it as a means to supreme power—"

The blur came back, and during the minutes that followed it was evident the cells were losing their unity of personality. Wild cells remained, bewildered groups, masses of neurons, holding their separate pictures unsteadily against the encroaching death. Finally, he caught another coherent thought:

". . . I discovered the galactic base, and visited the universe . . . I came back and superintended the construction of the Games Machine—only a computer could in the beginning control the undisciplined hordes that lived on earth. And it was I who chose Venus as the planet where men of null-A could be free. And then, despite my loss of memory—my injury—I was able to start growing bodies again other than those of my own genera—genera—"

That was all he got. Minutes and minutes passed, and there was only an occasional blur. Gosseyn climbed at last to his feet. He felt the glowing excitement of a man who had triumphed over death itself. But it was too bad that the vital information of body duplication had not surfaced. Except for that and one other thing, he was satisfied. The other thing: He had, he realized, allowed one meaning to slide by him. But, now, it came to the fore, with its implications: ". . . *Between your group and mine the continuity was broken!*"

Odd, how all these minutes, that had not really penetrated. The idea of a connection was so remote in his mind; his earlier rejection of "X" so complete. And yet—

the continuity could only be, could only refer to . . . memory. Besides, who else could he be?

Feverishly, he went in search of shave salve. He found a jar in a washroom down the hall. With trembling fingers, he rubbed it over the beard of the still, dead face.

The beard came off easily into a towel. Gosseyn knelt there looking down at a face that was older than he had thought, seventy-five, possibly eighty years old. It was an unmistakable face, and of itself answered many questions. Here beyond all argument was the visible end-reality of his search.

The face was his own.

MORE EXCITING S. F. FROM BERKLEY